I0717982

# Mel Goes to Hell

DEMELZA CARLTON

# DEDICATION

For Opa, who made an angel swear in Heaven
while I was writing this book. She must have
spent all day preparing his place up there –
only for him to decide he was staying on Earth
for a bit longer.

# One

Soft lips brushed his cheek. Luce turned his head to claim a kiss for his mouth, too, but met only air. He opened his eyes, searching for the source of the soft kisses, just in time to see her back depart through the doorway.

He glanced at the room, taking a moment to remember the events of the previous night. Persephone, signing the contracts, before he left in the downpour...

He scrambled out of bed, trying not to make a sound before he made sure his memories were accurate.

"You know how you owe me a favour?" Mel's lovely voice said.

Luce's breath caught in his throat as he walked faster. He needed to see her to be sure.

She was talking on the telephone, resting her forearm on the bench so she could lean across it. One ankle was crossed behind the other, her toes tapping lightly on the carpet. Luce stood transfixed at this vision.

Mel had invited him in, given him a spectacular kiss, before demonstrating that she was heavenly in more ways than he'd imagined.

"Don't worry. Persi is aware of her mistake and she won't make it again. If he finds you, don't let him in – call us and we'll take care of him. It's hardly a favour – just us protecting a valuable member of our staff," a muffled male voice sounded through the phone line.

Mel's caller was talking about him, Luce realised. Not to let him in, because he was the mistake. But Mel had, and she'd taken better care of him than anyone else would or could. She was the best kind of angel.

"No, it's not that," Mel replied. "Look, can I

meet with you in person, some time this morning? I'd prefer to discuss this face to face."

"I have a meeting at nine, but I'm free from ten. How about then?" the voice said.

She turned to look at the clock above Luce's head. He didn't have time to hide himself or conceal how he'd been staring at her, so he brazened it out, meeting her eyes when her glance lowered to his face, before her gaze dropped lower still.

"Ten sounds fine. See you then," she said, turning away from Luce.

Sprung, Luce didn't waste time. He strode across the carpet to Mel, reaching out to touch her. "You should've told him it's too late – I've already found you," he whispered, feeling her tense up. She dropped the phone on the counter, letting Luce see that she'd ended the call.

"I'd like to keep you to myself for a little longer, first. I'm not sure what I've done to you and it wouldn't be fair to desert you so soon," Mel admitted.

Luce's heart sank. "So I'm under

observation, like some sort of medical case, Mel? Not because you feel something for me, except maybe morbid curiosity?" he asked bitterly. He glanced up at the clock. "And you'll discharge me at ten, when you have a meeting with a secretive somebody who thinks I'm a mistake."

Steel-strong hands grasped his as her eyes bored into his soul. "You're coming with me to that meeting. Afterwards, I'll be all yours. After all, we're both unemployed. Perhaps you should start thinking about what we'll do together."

Luce's mind whirled. Together. All his. Mel.

"So what would you like for breakfast?" she asked.

Luce chuckled. "You – or, failing that, anything else you're willing to offer." He pressed his lips lightly to her neck, praying that she wouldn't pull away as he drew a deep draught of her scent. Heaven. She smelled of Heaven – or did Heaven smell of her?

"You are a sexy devil, aren't you?" Mel laughed, shaking her head.

Luce shrugged. "I have no idea what I am

now, but still sexy, I'm sure."

# Two

Mel filled the kettle and clicked it on, but nothing happened. She flicked the switch a couple of times, with no result. Next, she tried to switch on the kitchen light – unnecessary with the bright morning sunlight streaming in – but that didn't work, either. "The power must still be out from last night," Mel murmured, frowning.

"The power's out? When did that happen?" Luce asked. "Must have slept through that."

"No," Mel said softly. "We did it. We...blew

the transformer when we kissed. I hope it isn't too much trouble to repair. I'll have to remember not to redeem demons in the house again if it is." She smiled, but Luce thought she looked a little sad, too. "How are you feeling this morning?"

"Better than I have in years," Luce admitted, grinning. "A couple more nights like last night and I'll feel like the king of the world again." The look of horror on Mel's face made him realise what he'd said. He held up both hands in surrender. "I mean that in a purely metaphorical sense. I gave that up – I swear."

Mel nodded gravely, but she still didn't seem convinced.

"Look, let me make you breakfast. A small thank you for everything you've done for me. Power-hungry demons don't make you breakfast, right?"

"What are you going to make, given that the power's out? I can't even make tea," she said.

Luce eyed the gas stove. "Where do you keep your pots and pans?"

Mel pointed at the cupboard beside the stove. Luce rummaged through it until he found a saucepan and a frypan. He filled the pot with water before setting both on the stove. He turned the control knobs for the burners, hearing the hiss of gas but not the click of the igniter.

"The ignition is electric," Mel said. "It won't work."

"Maybe not for an angel like you, but I've been playing with fire for a very long time," Luce said grimly, touching his index fingers to the gas jets. Both burst into brilliant blue flame. He scooped a tiny flickering tongue of flame onto his fingertip, lifting it to show Mel. She stared at it as if mesmerised.

"Angels can't do that," she said softly, looking worried. "Luce..."

He laughed and blew out the flame. "Maybe I'm not entirely redeemed after all." He peered into his pants. "Yep, I'm still up for a bit of action on the couch – and I am seriously hot." A wisp of smoke curled up from his extinguished finger.

Mel laughed, but her heart didn't seem in it. She was hiding something, Luce decided, but there was no point in trying to push it out of her. It must be something to do with her early morning phone call.

"So what are you making me for breakfast?" she asked.

"Got eggs and milk? Mushrooms, bacon, ham, cheese...anything I can fold into an omelette?"

"I have all but the bacon," Mel said warmly, opening the dark fridge.

Together, they laid out the ingredients for a decadent omelette, before Luce insisted that Mel sit down and let him do the work. She laughed a little but acquiesced, settling into one of the dining chairs in the alcove just beyond the kitchen.

Luce opened the tiny tin of mushrooms and drained it. He started slicing them, pausing occasionally to smile at the watching angel.

The longer he looked, the more he saw. Mel wasn't beautiful in a classic or a modern sense, so she didn't stand out. She wasn't ugly, either – he'd call her pretty. Her form fitted the soul it contained, sure, for her radiant smile shone through that face like the sun itself. He wondered why she hadn't chosen a more striking body — it was almost as if she were trying to blend in or hide among humans. An angel with power like hers faced little danger from anyone. What or who could she possibly be hiding from?

He became aware of a stinging pain in his finger. "Ow...oh shit!" Instead of cutting a mushroom, he'd hacked off half his own fingertip. Red blood was leaking across the cutting board, creeping closer to the mushrooms.

Luce stared in fascination. He hadn't seen red blood flow from his veins since...since the night he fell. The blows from Michael's sword had burned as they cut, and he could remember seeing his own blood on his hands. The last thing he saw before he fell...and his blood had been black ever since. Until now.

"Luce. It's all right," Mel soothed, her hands prying the knife from his. His blood tainted her fingers, yet she didn't shrink from it.

He tried to pull his hand away, his mind whirling at what to do. Hospital. He should get to a hospital, where they'd be able to stitch his finger back together. Before he lost too much blood.

Mel's fingers felt like steel – stronger than any set of handcuffs he owned – yet her hands were smaller and slimmer than his. He couldn't break her grip, even as she brought her other hand toward his severed finger. Sickened, he saw the bone between the blood and tissue, before her hand hid his from sight. Some of the salt had seeped into the wound and the stinging became unbearable.

"Stop," he gasped. "Please. Take me to hospital. Need some painkillers and they can fix this."

"Kiss me," Mel murmured. "It will help."

Luce snorted. "How?" Half the word was swallowed by her lips connecting with his. His whole hand was on fire and her kiss was just a pleasant distraction, but not enough. Tears of pain coursed down his cheeks – he could taste the salt and he was sure Mel could, too, but she continued to kiss him as she kept his hand captive.

He broke away from her. "Mel. Please..." He was embarrassed to hear it come out sounding like a sob. It felt like his hand was going numb from the blood loss – or was it Mel's strong grip?

"Here, let me wash the blood away so I can get a better look," she said, pulling him toward the sink. Cool water trickled across his skin and he didn't dare look at the damage, though it wasn't hurting as much. Perhaps the water had numbed it further.

She forced his injured hand up between them, level with her lips. She started to kiss his fingers. First his thumb, then his index finger. He felt the touch of her tongue on the tip of his middle finger, dreading the pain when she touched his next, injured finger.

"Mel, please, stop," he begged. This was worse than the humiliation Persephone put him through. But Mel was an angel, the kindest he'd ever met. She wouldn't hurt him like this...

He felt another tear slip out of the corner of his eye as he squeezed them tightly shut, the tiniest defence against the pain he knew was coming.

Her lips grazed his pinkie, then pulled away. He could feel her breath on his hand as she said, "Open your eyes, Luce."

He knew what was next, but he heard the command in her tone and he had to obey. He couldn't not do it. Her fingers shielded his, so he couldn't see the last joint of his finger just hanging, blood trickling... He felt his knuckle graze her lips and wondered what in Hell she was doing.

"But you're an angel. An angel, Mel. Please..."

She set his finger alight as she gently sucked on the length of it, from base to tip. He fancied he could feel her tongue tickling his injured fingertip, but that wasn't possible – he'd seen the severed nerve. He'd seen...

He saw her pull his finger from her mouth, whole and healed as if it had never happened. He'd been able to heal when he was an angel, but never as fast or as perfectly as this. "How?" he gasped.

Her eyes held him. "Love, Luce. When you love someone, you'd do anything for them. Take away their pain. Heal their hurts. Lift them when they fall. Help them when they need you most. Love is my greatest strength, Luce, and I love you." There was power in her voice – he was under no illusions that it was anyone less than Muriel of the Hashmallim who had him mesmerised.

Giddy from the blood loss, misty-eyed at the heavy attraction for both Mel and the power she held over him, Luce couldn't think straight. He didn't have to. He seized her in an embrace that would have crushed a weaker woman. Not Mel. Her body was firm against him – not resisting, but not compliant, either. His kiss was clumsy and rough, but she responded as if he'd been skilful and seductive, for she was both.

He wanted her...oh Hell, how he wanted her. Blearily, he peered over her shoulder at the couch. He wouldn't make it that far. Maybe if he lifted her onto the bench...His back slammed into the fridge and he forgot about the bench. Mel's body pinned his to the metal and it didn't matter where as long as it was now. Oh God, MEL...

She released him and he almost fell. He stared at her, hurt. What had he done wrong?

"The water's boiling and we should probably turn both burners off if we're not going to use them," Mel said, wiping her mouth with her hand. She looked as flushed as he felt, but her grin showed no guilt.

Luce glanced at the stove. The water was boiling over – hissing into steam as it threatened to extinguish the burner flame beneath it. How had he missed the sound?

"I'll make us some tea and you make breakfast. We need to get into the city for that meeting at ten," Mel said, regret in her tone.

"And maybe later we can finish what we started?" Luce asked eagerly.

"Yes. Later, Luce." The look she gave him held unmistakeable love. No one had ever looked at him like that before.

His heart swelled in his chest. Miracles did happen. He was an angel again and Mel loved HIM.

# Three

Dressed in his still slightly damp suit, Luce slid into his car. He'd parked it halfway up Mel's street, in the only available spot, but the walk seemed a lot shorter now in dry daylight with Mel by his side. He couldn't keep the smile off his face as she climbed into the passenger seat beside him.

Her eyes were serious. "If you drive like a maniac, I will get out and walk. You only get one warning."

He winked. "Yes, ma'am. I'll be the

smoothest chauffeur you ever had, I swear. I'll have you naked in the back seat before you can —"

"Luce. That really is enough."

He waited for her to click her seatbelt into place over her pale grey suit skirt before he pulled his black Jaguar smoothly out of the tight space, letting his blissful mood infuse his driving. He was in no hurry.

Mel watched the traffic as he drove, occasionally glancing at him but shifting her gaze before he could meet her eyes. He wondered what he'd missed of her telephone conversation before he'd interrupted and what sort of favour she'd be asking for – and from whom.

He turned into the HELL Corporation garage entrance, swiping his passcard to open the gate as he nodded to the guard. He drove automatically to his personal car bay on the second level down, only to stop in shock as he saw it occupied by a bright yellow smart car.

"Persi's car," Mel said.

Luce yanked the steering wheel around and parked his car in the general HELL

Corporation space beside the tiny irritant in his parking spot. He sat glowering at it and all it symbolised, before realising that Mel stood outside his door, waiting. He hurried to get out so she wouldn't leave without him, but she didn't seem to be in a hurry. He locked the car and turned on the alarm at a touch. Mel extended her hand toward him.

He held out the keys, unsure. "What do you want?" An unfamiliar desire to give her anything she asked for swept over him, confusing him even more.

She smiled gently. "Your hand, Luce. I'd like to walk down the street, holding your hand, if you don't mind. I don't keep secrets easily – I prefer an open declaration, where possible."

He shoved the keys in his pocket and grabbed her hand. "Let's go."

Mel's laughter echoed through the underground car park, but Luce liked the sound. There was no cruelty in it – she laughed for joy, he knew.

As they stepped out onto the street, joining the crowds of commuters hurrying to or from coffee shops for their mid-morning caffeine hit, Luce gave in and asked, "Where are we headed?"

"The agency that employs me," Mel responded, glancing at the traffic before stepping out onto the road. "Raphael owes me a favour or three and I think today is an ideal occasion to cash in."

"You mean the Helpful Angels Agency? I'm not going to be very welcome there," Luce admitted. "I could just camp out in a coffee shop somewhere and wait for you to come rejoin me so I can buy you one. It might be easier."

Mel's fingers tightened around his. "Oh, no. You're coming in with me – whatever they think and say. You have a right to be there, as the favour I'll ask for involves you – intimately, I think. They need to know how serious I am about this and your very presence will help to emphasise that."

She sounded like she was planning for battle – a battle she'd surely win. "If you'd accepted my offer to be my PA instead of Persephone, nothing could have stopped us. With you at my side, I bet I'd never have been thrown out of Heaven," Luce blurted out.

Mel glanced at Luce, pressing her lips together. "Perhaps," she said, picking up the pace so he had to hurry to keep up.

He almost missed the doorway, which was set between two shops, with the winged HAA logo stencilled on the glass. Luckily, Mel didn't let go of him as she seized the doorknob with her free hand, leading Luce up the stairs behind her.

At least he got a nice view of her arse to bolster him up the stairs – a small, unexpected slice of Heaven, Luce decided, slowing his ascent to make the most of it.

# Four

"Good morning, Mel! It's wonderful to see you," a warm voice greeted her. "We've been so worried..."

Luce couldn't see the girl's face yet, but he doubted he'd get such an enthusiastic greeting. Hell, he'd never heard one like it at HELL Corporation, either. As his head rose above the banister, he got a clear view of the receptionist. He recognised Gabrielle instantly.

Mel's grip tightened around his fingers, so he plastered a grin on his face as he pounded up the last few stairs to the landing. "This is my friend, Luce. He'll be coming in to see Raphael with me at ten," Mel said with a beaming smile.

Gabrielle's smile turned to a look of horror. "Mel, that's...that's..."

Flashing a smile and a wink to the archangel receptionist, Luce held out his hand to shake Gabrielle's. "Luce Iblis, recently retired CEO of the HELL Corporation. I'm sure you've worked under me in our office." Gabrielle hid her hands beneath the desk, so he reached for Mel's hand instead, pulling her fingers to his lips. "Mel has kindly arranged a meeting for me with Raphael." From the corner of his eye, he could see Mel's professional smile, giving nothing away. Mel could hide more secrets with her open, angelic smile than he held in all of Hell, Luce mused.

Gabrielle jumped up from her desk. "I'll go see if he's through with his nine o'clock," she said breathlessly, hurrying in her heels to one of the enclosed offices along the back wall.

"Shall we sit?" he asked Mel, waving at the sofa against the wall. Mel nodded and followed him to the seat. She carefully placed herself on the cushions so her skirt sat perfectly, then waited for Luce to take the other half of the couch. He wasn't as worried about appearances as she seemed to be – he stretched out his arms as he relaxed into the white leather, one along the armrest and the other around Mel. She straightened her back the tiniest bit, but didn't move to push him away.

Both were silent as they heard panicked voices from the office with the partially closed door – it appeared that Gabrielle had forgotten to close it.

A male voice said, "She's here. By some miracle, she made it through the night without him finding her. He's probably hunting her now – I'll keep her safe, I swear. If I have the whole agency guarding her, I'll find somewhere to hide her that he'll never think to look. Find me some crisis on the other side of the world we can use to coerce her to leave. North Korea, Canada, UK, Siberia, Ukraine...there has to be something. Find out and call back within the hour, while she's still here." The phone rattled into its cradle, as if the man's hands were shaking. Gabrielle's voice murmured quietly – too low for him to discern the words. Luce figured they were probably about him, anyway.

"Wherever you go, I want to come with you," Luce whispered and Mel nodded. He wondered what she was agreeing to – his company or just his desire? His thoughts were interrupted by movement across the office.

Raphael emerged behind Gabrielle, his face whiter than his shirt. His eyes flicked briefly to Luce, but his attention was on Mel. "Please, God, no," he whispered, just loud enough to carry to Luce's ears.

Luce wondered what he was so worried about. Did the angel think he'd managed to corrupt Mel? The world would end before he'd succeed at that – which sounded good to him.

"Mel, I'm so sorry about the imposition on you, particularly when you're on leave. I'd like to discuss it with you privately, if possible," Raphael said, not acknowledging Luce at all.

Before Mel could respond, Luce chimed in, "Fine by me. If you have company secrets to discuss, I'll just sit out here and keep Gabrielle company. Keep her from getting lonely and all." He grinned at the receptionist, who blanched as she sank onto her desk chair.

"Gabi won't be alone for long, Luce. I'm sure she's just holding the fort until everyone else returns with coffee. It might be best for everyone if you're not sitting at the top of the stairs when a whole pack of coffee-carrying Grigori come up." She lifted her eyes to Raphael. "It's fine. What I'm here to discuss can be said in front of Luce."

Raphael evidently didn't agree, but he also didn't seem to want to argue with Mel, so he gestured toward his office, leading the way. He offered them both a seat before hurrying around the desk to put its laminated width between them.

Luce wanted to laugh at how nervously these angels seemed to treat him, as if he might explode at any moment, but he didn't want to embarrass Mel. He was as eager as Raphael seemed to be to hear what she had to say.

"How are you, Mel? Are you well?" Raphael began, staring at her with worried eyes. "You didn't experience any damage last night in the storm?" He seemed to be searching for a reply without saying what he really sought.

"I'm fine," Mel said, her serene smile speaking volumes to Luce that Raphael didn't seem to understand.

"Are you sure? Nothing different at all?" Raphael persisted.

Luce lost patience. "By all that's holy, I haven't corrupted the girl. I showed up at her house last night in the storm, with nothing but my car and the soaked clothes I stood up in. Mel was kind enough to take me in and let me stay until the storm was over. Your precious angel is as pristine and perfect as I found her." He reached for the letter opener on Raphael's desk, which turned out to be surprisingly sharp – perfect for his needs. "The problem is THIS." He dragged the blade across his palm, and a line of ruby blood erupted.

Raphael's eyes widened. "How...? Demon blood is black. How can you have blood like ours?"

Mel touched her fingers to Luce's palm, causing the cut to close.

"Thank you," Luce said in surprise.

"Demons can't be healed by angels! What in Hell?" Raphael exclaimed, jumping up and backing into the wall, away from the sight before him.

"I'd say your precious angel has corrupted me into something like you."

"That's not possible!" Raphael replied. "Demons are damned, never to be redeemed!"

"If you have a better explanation, I'd love to hear it. Because I've got nothing," Luce snapped.

"What have you done?" Raphael stared at Mel, looking scared. "That's not just any demon you've changed. You've redeemed the Lord of Hell!"

"He came to me and begged for my help. I'd do no less for any other human and he seemed little more than that, with the power Persi stripped from him. He was shivering, standing on my front steps in a soaked suit." Mel shrugged. "What can I say? He makes a good cup of tea."

# Five

"You owe me a favour, Raphael," Mel stated. "I'd like to use it to clear up some of the mess resulting from this assignment."

"If you want him changed back into a demon, I'm sure Michael would be happy to help," Raphael replied eagerly.

"No!" Mel and Luce said together. Luce looked at her in surprise, but she had more to say.

"I want you to arrange an invitation for Luce to re-enter Heaven, Raphael. He's been kept out for long enough. I'm happy to explain his case up there in person, if required."

Both men stared at her.

"Michael won't be happy about this," Raphael said, shaking his head. "I should never have brought you in on this assignment. Now..."

"Michael's never happy," Mel replied abruptly, but she didn't elaborate.

Luce looked from one to the other, wondering what was going unsaid in this exchange. He hoped it was more about Michael's insecurities than anything to do with him. He'd never liked Michael, not after what he'd done to him. If Michael was miserable, that was fine by him. Served the righteous bastard right.

"It'll take some time and a lot of work, Mel. I'll find him somewhere to stay in the meantime," Raphael muttered, as if Luce wasn't sitting right in front of him. "It won't be up to his normal opulent standard, but if he's serious about joining our ranks, he'll just have to make do..."

"Luce, you're welcome to stay with me for

as long as you need to," Mel said.

That sounded pretty good to him. Luce cleared his throat. "Thank you."

"Michael really won't like that at all," Raphael said, looking even more worried.

Mel rose to her feet. "Michael isn't my keeper. Perhaps he needs to realise that there are some things he can't control." She bowed her head slightly to Raphael. "Thank you. Let me know when you have more to tell me."

Luce stood, too, opening the office door so they could leave the stuffy space.

"Mel, you know Michael's only trying to protect you," Raphael said urgently. "Don't let his charm win you over. Remember who and what he is."

Mel's voice was cold. "I know what Michael's trying to do and it wouldn't be necessary if he'd taken my advice, instead of picking and choosing the bits he liked best. I'm under no illusions about Luce. I wish I could say the same about Michael's perception of me."

Luce couldn't hide his smile. It sounded like Mel and Michael had a history that hadn't ended well. He swore he'd be better to her than that idiot of an overprotective archangel. Whatever it took.

# Six

Luce tried not to show how relieved he felt to hear the HAA door close behind them as they reached the street. "Would you like to grab a coffee or maybe an early lunch?" he asked Mel.

"Sure," she said.

They headed to a nearby café, where they both ordered coffee before sitting at a table at the very back. Partway between the coffee rush and the lunch rush, Luce knew the café's emptiness wouldn't last, but they could take advantage of it while it did.

Luce opened his mouth to ask Mel about her relationship with Michael.

"Gah! That was a bloody waste of time," a loud, male voice complained. Timber creaked as the man sat down at the table beside Luce and Mel.

"No, it wasn't. Those suits were perfect. You'll match the bridesmaids and the flowers, so it'll be a real wedding to remember. Just think of the photos..." the girl said dreamily as she sat in the chair across from him.

Mel covered her smile, clearly trying not to laugh. She evidently knew more about this couple and their wedding than Luce did.

"I AM thinking of the photos – we'll have them for the rest of our lives. I'm not getting married in a hot pink suit!" the man protested.

Luce burst out laughing.

The girl glared at Luce, then pursed her mouth as she turned her eyes back to her fiancé. "I thought you'd do anything for me. Now you won't even wear the suit I want you to at our wedding. Maybe you don't want to marry me at all." She rose to her full height, which would barely have reached Luce's chest.

She gave a little snort and a nod, before turning her back on her fiancé to stride angrily out of the café.

Mel reached over and touched the man's arm. "Tell her you would do anything for her. Swim through sharks, give your life to save hers," she whispered.

The man pulled his arm irritably away from Mel as he stood up. Luce felt bad for her – she'd only tried to help, after all. He hoped she wouldn't be hurt. After all, humans weren't known for taking advice from strangers and maybe the bloke was better off without his bridezilla.

"Jess, I would do almost anything for you!" the man shouted. "I'd swim through a school of sharks at Trigg Beach to get to you. I'd fend off an entire gang of bikies if they threatened to hurt you."

The girl stopped and turned around.

Luce recovered from his shock quickly. "Say you'd walk through Hell for her," he suggested. "Naked."

The bloke stared at him. "That's a fucking crazy idea. Who'd walk through Hell naked?"

He turned back to Jess. "And I'd marry you in my birthday suit on Swanbourne Beach if that's what you want, but if I make my brothers and my best mate wear pink suits, they'll kill me before the wedding!"

Some of the other café patrons started cheering and Jess sported a hot pink blush. "I couldn't get married on Swanbourne Beach. I've already ordered my dress and my underwear..."

The bloke shoved his way through tables to get to her and the cheering grew louder as the couple kissed. They left without ordering.

Luce turned back to Mel to find her staring at him. "What?"

"Who would walk through Hell naked?" she asked.

Luce shrugged. "I do it all the time. Well, usually with the horns, the tail, the red skin...you know, the whole works. People seem to expect it on occasion. Keeps the other demons in order, but clothes would just spoil the effect..." He broke off as he heard the rattle of crockery.

"Your coffee?" a frightened-looking waitress

stammered, the tray shaking in her hands.

# Seven

Luce's espresso contrasted nicely with Mel's macchiato, he thought. She hadn't seen his wings yet, though she'd certainly seen the rest of him last night. He'd been proud to be able to please an angel with his physique, when she was so accustomed to angelic perfection. She'd certainly appreciated his technique, too...

"Luce," Mel called. It sounded like it wasn't the first time, either.

Luce focussed on her face, trying not to remember what it looked like in her more passionate moments – like this morning. He could inspire her to remind him later. "Yes?"

"I asked what you wanted to do this afternoon. Given both of us are unemployed and relatively free, for the moment – your call." Mel smiled.

Luce thought he'd like to get her out of her conservative clothes and show her the devil of a good time. He'd happily do that all afternoon and into the evening, too.

"Clothes?" Mel asked.

Luce stared at her. Had she read his mind? He'd heard there were angels who could read thoughts and his had been fairly graphic. He felt a blush colour his cheeks. "What about clothes?" he ventured.

"Don't you need more clothes? All you have are your current suit and shirt. You're going to need fresh ones for tomorrow."

Luce shrugged. "I can buy some more before we leave, I guess." He tried not to show how relieved he felt.

Mel shook her head, still smiling. Luce didn't want her to stop smiling – ever. "I assume Persephone made you sign over your house, along with everything else, but she'd have no use for your clothes. Wouldn't it be easier just to ask her if you can have them?"

When Mel put it so reasonably, it sounded like the easiest thing in the world – but she couldn't know Persephone as well as he did. The half-angel, which he suspected was also half-demon, would probably insist he do something incredibly degrading for every single sock. He still had horrible flashbacks about her tattoo. Hundreds of damned, writhing, naked...all scrambling and fighting to get closer to her unholy halo...

"Do you want me to call her and ask for you?" Mel asked kindly – once again, as if she could read his mind.

Luce shivered and said, "I'd really appreciate it if you would. Buying new might be easier, though."

Mel pulled out her phone and made the call. After less than a minute of speaking to Persephone, she ended the conversation. She turned her eyes to Luce again. "She said you can have all of your clothes, shoes, accessories and toiletries. I'd like to smell your aftershave on you again." She slipped her phone into her bag. "We can go over there this afternoon while no one's home, if you still have your house keys. Otherwise, we can go pick up the keys from her in the office."

"I still have my keys, so we can do it without having to see her. Thank you – for everything," Luce said, dazed. "What did she ask for in return?" He dreaded knowing, but he knew he needed to.

Mel laughed. "Persi is deeply in my debt for giving out my phone number and address to a demon without my permission. She wouldn't dare ask me for anything until long after she's made reparation for that."

She'd been giving Mel's details out to random demons? Luce's hands clenched, ready for combat. "If any demon comes near your house..."

Mel laid her fingers gently over his fists. "There was only one demon – you, Luce. I'm sure we can come to some sort of arrangement for me calling in a favour on your behalf."

"In other words, I'll be in your debt?" he suggested. "Even deeper than I am already, of course."

"That sounds tempting. In the meantime — it's time for you to show me where you lived, Luce."

He thought of his Crawley penthouse. "With pleasure."

# Eight

"There's the restaurant I wanted to take you to on Valentine's Day," Luce said, pointing. "Really fresh oysters..." He stopped. "Sorry, I know you don't like oysters." He didn't think she'd heard him as she didn't respond.

Mel's curiosity was clear in her wide eyes as she followed him into the old brewery by the river. "How long have you lived here?"

"I bought this apartment off the plans. Why?"

"Well, this bit of land has a reputation for

being cursed. Apparently, there's a huge snake that lies in wait for the unwary here. I'm just wondering how much you had to do with the origin of that particular legend..." Mel wore her wicked smile, the one Luce found hard to believe he was seeing on an angel's face.

"Big snake? Sounds like my style," Luce replied, wondering just how much Mel knew about him. She had said she knew his history, but realisation dawned on him that she could have meant far more than his initial fall from Heaven. In contrast, he knew almost nothing about her.

How was that possible? There weren't that many angels as old as she was – and he knew a fair bit about all of the others. He'd fought with or against all of them in the past. Given she was still an angel and hadn't fallen with him, she must have been one of those against him, but he knew he'd never seen her before she'd walked into the HELL Corporation offices. It was almost as if she'd been deliberately avoiding him – or hidden from him by someone else.

Worried, he shoved the key into the lock

and almost broke it off as he wrenched it around. The key twisted and unlocked the door, but he hesitated before opening it for Mel. The view from the arched windows was absolutely stunning, and he wanted her to enjoy it.

"Are you ready?" he asked.

"For what?" she replied.

He grinned. "Entering the devil's lair. I could have a den with whips, chains and all sorts of torture implements in here. Aren't you worried about what you might find? Or that you might not make it out?"

Her smile didn't waver as she looked deep into his eyes – no, into his soul, he realised. "You don't torture people for pleasure. You tease and torment, yes, but pain is reserved for those who you feel deserve it – those who have caused similar pain. I don't think you enjoy it, either – or you would never have left Hell. You could be hiding poor taste in decorating, though – the walls of your place might be plastered with naked pictures of all the women you've slept with." She laughed. "If that's the case, the worst you'll do to me is make me blush."

Now he was more worried than ever. She knew him almost as well as he knew himself – details he'd never really thought about, and she saw so much! What if she thought he had bad taste?

Mel's smile softened and she stopped laughing. "It's all right. If you really do have naked pictures on the wall, I'll do my best not to look, so I don't embarrass you. Oh...unless the naked pictures are of you?"

Luce laughed aloud. Why in Hell would he want to see naked pictures of himself? "Okay, just as long as you feel you're ready." He threw the door wide open and strode in, beckoning her to follow him. He stood beside the windows, his eyes fixed on her and not the view of Melville Water. "What do you think?" he asked anxiously.

"The view is really beautiful. You can almost see clear to my place from here." She turned sympathetic eyes from the panorama to him. "It must have been hard to give this place up."

He'd never really thought about it until now – this place wasn't his any more. Instead, he had Mel. Or he'd had her for a night. Cautiously, he laid an arm around her shoulders, wondering if she'd pull away, even as he pulled her to him. His relief hissed out with his breath as she rested her head against his chest.

"It was worth it," he responded. "I mean, you or a big snake. The choice was easy."

She laughed. "I know what I'd prefer." She didn't enlighten him. Instead, she said, "We should really start packing up your clothes, or we'll still be here when Persi gets home. I don't think I've ever seen you wear the same black shirt twice, until today. It'll take us a while to get them all packed."

She'd noticed. He felt absurdly gratified to hear it. He wondered what else she'd noticed but feigned indifference to.

"C'mon, Luce. You won't shock me with your extensive wardrobe. I've seen you wear a lot of it at work." Mel stepped away from him, headed for his bedroom. He hurried to follow, hoping he hadn't left any of his sex toys out where Mel could find them. Or worse – if Persephone had found them after he'd left.

How could he explain his handcuff collection to an angel like Mel?

47

# Nine

Countless trips later, he'd filled the car with his clothes, shoes and other personal items. He'd managed to hide at least three sets of cuffs without Mel seeing, or at least, he hoped so. The pair weighing heavily in his coat pocket had featured prominently in a particularly elaborate fantasy about Mel. He didn't even want to contemplate Persephone touching them.

As he headed back up in the lift to the apartment one last time, Luce wondered whether his whiskeys counted as personal items. Persephone hated whiskey and some of the more mature ones would definitely be wasted on her. He'd ask Mel what she thought about taking the bottles. After all, she'd made the bargain with Persephone – she'd know whether the alcohol was included with his stuff.

He found her standing at his bedroom window, staring out across the water.

"Did you know you could see the dolphins from here?" Mel turned her eager eyes on him and held out her hand. "Come watch them play."

He took her hand, letting her reel him in, before dropping it to wrap his arms around her. Mel pointed at the fins cutting through the water, near Matilda Bay. They'd stroked the swans together on that shore and he'd wanted to bring her here ever since. "There," she said.

Luce peered out at them over her shoulder, then shrugged. "Are you sure those are dolphins? I always thought they were baby bull sharks. There are a fair few of them in the river."

Mel laughed. "No, the sharks are smaller, with different tails. They're far shyer, too. Look at their tails. Sharks swim with their tails flicking from side to side, like this" – she moved her hand to demonstrate – "and dolphins are mammals, so they undulate up and down, like this," she said, rippling her arm like the dolphins in the bay below.

"I should've had you up here a long time ago, just so you could tell me what I was seeing." Luce glanced at the bed. "I'd still be happy to have you here now. It's just us, my king-sized bed and the amazing view..."

Mel turned cold. "It's not your house or your bed any more, Luce. It all belongs to Persi. Even with the wonderful view, someone else's bed simply doesn't appeal to me. Have you packed up all your things? The car must be pretty full by now. I think you own more shoes than I do."

Luce felt his face redden. The way she said it, it sounded so sordid. Like offering her his dirty desk. Again, she was right. Persephone had cuffed herself to this bed and it was soiled by sheer association. It didn't even look like she'd changed the sheets. Hell, the whole penthouse was polluted by her presence, the venomous little viper. Now he wanted to leave more than Mel did. There were the whiskeys, though...

"I have all my clothes and shoes in the car. I was wondering about my whiskey. Do you think they count as personal items? Most of the bottles are opened," he said.

Mel tilted her head, considering. "Does Persi like whiskey?"

Luce laughed. "No. When we were in Japan last week, I was given some particularly fine bottles of Hibiki. She almost caused an incident when she choked on her first mouthful. I think the bottles are here somewhere..."

"I've never tasted Japanese whiskey, though I admit I'm quite fond of the Scottish ones. Something about the peat they use there. It's certainly improved a lot since the early batches in the 1500s, too. They called it the water of life back then, though." Mel nodded slowly. "If they fit into your car, you can take them. I'll arrange it with Persi when I speak to her next."

Mel liked whiskey? Luce brightened. He'd pack every single bottle he owned – and throw out all his shoes to make room in the car if he had to. Surely she'd appreciate the twenty-one-year-old Hibiki. He headed for the walk-in pantry behind the bar, where he kept his spirits.

# Ten

"Mel? Are you still here?"

Luce almost dropped his best bottle of Laphroaig at the sound of Persephone's voice. He tried to pull the door shut, so she wouldn't see him. But, because he couldn't close it completely without making noise, he still heard her clearly.

"I'm in the main bedroom, admiring the view," Mel called back.

"Oh, Mel, I'm so sorry! Raphael shouted at me so much last night that I cried! I should never have told him how to find you. It all seemed so easy, so simple, that I thought you wouldn't mind and Raphael was so angry. I didn't know..."

Was Raphael the one who'd tried to hide her from him? Luce wondered. Or was he just doing it now, for someone else? Whoever he'd been on the phone with this morning...

"It's all right," Mel's calm voice interrupted. "Have you spoken to Raphael yet today?"

Luce tried not to make a sound as he packed the remaining bottles into the box. He definitely didn't want her to know he was here.

Persephone's inane giggle set Luce's teeth on edge. "No! He'll only shout at me again and I didn't want to cry in front of all those demons at the office. Your call was a godsend. I couldn't leave you to pack up all the demon's things by yourself, so I got off work as early as I could and raced over here to help you. Do you want me to get started on the shoes? I've never known a man who had so many. I don't think I've met a man like him, ever. I still can't believe he wasn't the slightest bit interested in me — I even offered him his choice of handcuffs! Do you think it might be because he doesn't like women?"

Mel coughed to cover what Luce thought sounded more like laughter. He hoped she wasn't laughing about the handcuffs. "Maybe he just likes good shoes. Actually, most of Luce's things are already packed and downstairs. There's not really much more for you to do."

"Are you sure? You shouldn't have to deal with the demon's things like this. I definitely don't need any of them. Raphael should have sent some of the boys from the agency over to do it, or I would have when I got home. I'd have had a courier deliver them to...wherever Raphael wanted them. Are you sure there's nothing else I can do to help?"

"It's fine. Like I said, all taken care of. Oh, there was one thing I was wondering about. His whiskey. Would it be all right if I took that, too? It'd be a shame to waste it."

Luce held his breath, hoping. The little minx would probably pour them all down the drain if she knew they were for him and not just Mel.

"Take anything you want," Persephone said warmly. "He keeps the best alcohol in the cupboard behind the bar..."

Luce had only a moment's warning of her approach, but he had nowhere to go with the box of bottles in his arms. The door flew open – and Persephone's mouth did, too.

She pursed her lips almost immediately. "Mel, did you know the demon was hiding in the cupboard?" She glared at Luce, who backed up involuntarily. "You were going to jump her when she came to collect the whiskey, weren't you? If you hurt Mel, you'll have every angel in the agency, and Heaven as well, after your hide. If you so much as touch her, I will personally chop your willy off!"

Was he imagining it, or did her eyes look more red than brown for a moment there? Luce wondered, trying unobtrusively to cross his legs where he stood. Just in case.

"That won't be necessary, Persi," Luce heard Mel say. He tried not to show how relieved he felt. "I brought Luce over to pack his own things. He can carry the whiskey down to the car for me, too." She pulled Persephone out of the way, so Luce had space to edge out of the cupboard, using the box as a shield between his body and the angry half-angel.

He hurried out of the apartment with the bottles, then took his time carrying it to the car park and loading it into the car. He debated whether to wait for Mel in the car or return upstairs to his former home and PA, wishing he didn't have to see Persephone again. Still, he knew he'd have to face her at some point.

Gah, when did she change from being simply a nuisance to something that scared him? As if her touch tainted him, when all he wanted was Mel. Who was waiting for him upstairs.

He sighed and trudged back up to the apartment, hoping Persephone would leave before he made it there.

"Mel, you really should let some of the Grigori boys take care of him. I should never have let him leave. Should have asked Michael to send him back to Hell where he belongs so he can't..." Persephone broke off abruptly as Luce shouldered past her to wrap an arm around Mel. He needed her like a lifeline.

"Are you ready to go?" he asked her, doing his damnedest to ignore the half-angel. "If we leave now, we can beat the peak-hour traffic and I can have everything put away at your place before dinner. I know this wonderful little seafood restaurant down by the water that serves the best oysters..." He grinned.

"I'm not eating oysters," Mel objected.

Luce let his grin widen. "You won't have to. I'll happily eat enough for both of us. You can order whatever you like and I'll drive you home after."

Mel's face lit with a genuine smile. "That sounds lovely." Her fingers closed around his. "See you later, Persi, and thank you for the whiskey."

Together, they walked out of the apartment, leaving a shocked Persephone behind them.

# Eleven

"These old wardrobes must've been built when people only owned a few clothes. It won't shut!" Luce grumbled.

Mel appeared in the doorway, the empty whiskey box in her arms. "Here. You take the box out to the recycling bin and I'll see if I can help. You can always put some of them in my wardrobe if you have to. I'm sure I have space for more."

Luce agreed and left her to it. He'd never had to deal with furniture that fought back before.

He returned to the guest room to find Mel squeezing through the doorway with an armload of his clothes. "Let me help," he said instantly, taking them from her.

"They'll have to go in my room. This one's full." Mel nodded at the now-closed wardrobe that housed his clothes and shoes.

He dumped his load on her bed and opened Mel's wardrobe door. It was pitifully bare – she had perhaps a dozen items hanging from the rail. Hell, he had more clothes on the bed. He recognised all of them, too – that one she'd worn to work on Melbourne Cup day; there was the suit she'd worn to her job interview, beside the skirt she'd worn on Valentine's Day. And the suit she'd worn on the day of the alien press conference, when she'd ended up as the HELL Corporation heroine. No, wait...there was one dress he'd never seen her wear. The shimmer of silk as it caught the light made him certain of it. He'd have dropped to his knees and begged if she had. An angel in deep gold silk...the gift!

"I got you a present while I was away. I

forgot to give it to you last night," Luce said, leaving his clothes where they lay to look for his suitcase. He knew he'd left it...ah, there it was. The box was slightly squashed at the corners, but the contents looked like they were intact. No leaking liquid or anything. Luce returned to Mel's room and held out the misshapen box. "For you."

Mel's eyes lit up as she looked at the package and carefully took it from his hands. "Thank you." She kissed him, but it was over so quickly that Luce barely had time to respond. He watched her peel off the crumpled plastic wrap and open the box. "How did you know?" she exclaimed, staring at him in wonder. She pulled out the bottle of perfume, holding it over her wrist in anticipation.

"You wore it every day at work. I came to see if you were free for lunch a few times, but you weren't at your desk. Once, there was this scent...like I'd just missed you and you'd sprayed your perfume on before you went out. I went through your desk drawers and then your filing cabinet, looking for it. I found it, but the bottle was almost empty. When I saw the same perfume in an airport duty-free shop, I had to get it. I wanted to give it to you...but I also wanted to keep it to remember you by." He closed his eyes, determined not to look at her. He sounded like some sappy romance hero, instead of the stern Lord of Hell. "Every day I was away, I thought of you. Wished it was you with me instead of that...that..."

"Lamprey?" Mel suggested.

"Yes!" Luce exclaimed. "You don't know what it was like. I mean, first it was just the short skirts and skimpy tops so I could look at the goods, as if she wanted me to ask how much she wanted for them. Then she left buttons and zips undone, like she wanted to take it all off. Then the constant offers. Sex, sex and more sex. She started offering with her clothes on, but they came off quickly. First, she wore those skimpy little French knickers, then switched to stringier and skimpier things until she left off underwear completely. Any excuse and she'd bend over to pick something up, flash that horrible tattoo and give a coy smile or a wink, like she thought I wanted to see what she had between her legs. I couldn't eat or drink anything when she was around, because I knew I wouldn't be able to keep it down when she dropped her fork again...Oh, Mel, you have no idea. I shuddered at the sight or sound of her – my own secretary! Not being able to get any work done around her, because of the constant offers of sex..."

Mel's gentle smile looked sympathetic. "Actually, I do. Some demons are more subtle than others, but your office had plenty of men who deemed themselves my prospective partners. One was particularly persistent."

"The demons at work hounded you like that half-angel pursued me? I'll send them all back to Hell in disgrace. I had no idea. You'll never have to see any of them again, I swear..."

"I don't work there any more and neither do you, so it's not really an issue now. And it wasn't as difficult for me as it was for you. I knew I could never accept any of the offers. I didn't want to hurt anyone, is all. As long as you were a demon, the most I was ever willing to offer you was dinner." Mel's smile turned sad and she turned away, busying herself with his clothes on the bed.

"You agreed to dinner tonight," Luce reminded her, starting to feel uneasy.

"I did," she said. She started hanging his shirts beside her dresses, pushing her meagre wardrobe aside to make more room for his. She stopped to finger the last one. "I've never seen you wear this to work."

Luce looked at the silk shirt that had caught her interest. "That's because I bought it in New York and I didn't trust my PA to get it dry-cleaned properly, so I haven't worn it yet. But for you, if you like...I'll wear it to dinner." He made swift work of his buttons, stripping off his shirt so he could change. "Or I could just go topless, for your viewing pleasure." He grinned, spreading his arms in an open invitation.

Mel laughed heartily as she stepped closer. "Are they real?" she asked, caressing his rippled muscles with her fingertips. It felt...indescribably good.

"All real. All...yours." He pulled her closer, wishing his pants didn't feel so tight. Maybe he should take them off, too. "And there's more,

Mel." He kicked his pants away from the puddle they'd formed around his ankles. For a moment, he wondered if her silence was because he was being too pushy, like he'd been in the office. Could he ever do the right thing around her? "But only if you want me," he said, hoping.

"Before or after dinner?" She gave his lips a light kiss.

"Both, if you like. An aperitif, then dinner, followed by a decadent dessert. I want to treat you like you deserve, Mel. You've done so much for me and I want to repay you in any way I can." Luce waved at himself before gesturing more broadly. "Me. The world. I'd give you anything, Mel. All you have to do is ask."

"I don't need you to give me the world. For now, you're enough," she said, giving him a deeper, more heavenly kiss.

"And after?" Luce's voice growled, to his surprise. He'd never heard himself sound so feral. Like some lust-crazed human about to jump her without her permission. But he wouldn't. Not Mel. After so many weeks without her, he needed to know she wouldn't leave him. She'd laugh if she knew, he was sure of it. The Lord of Hell, lost without Mel.

"You promised me dinner and dessert, my love. I'll hold you to that," Mel said, smiling. "Now show me what you have in mind for an aperitif."

# Twelve

She wore white – an angel in the kitchen, contrasting with the honey-coloured timber cabinets. Her hair was pinned up as it usually was in the office, baring her neck so that it fairly begged him for a kiss. He couldn't refuse her, so he moved as quietly as he could until she was close enough to touch. Maybe he hadn't used up all his oyster influence last night...

"What is it about white that makes you look so angelic?" he murmured as he kissed her neck.

Mel jumped and gave a yelp. Liquid splattered on the bench.

Luce lifted his head and realised she'd been handling hot tea. She moved quickly to the sink, running her red hands under the cold tap.

"I'm sorry, Mel. I didn't realise..." he began, wishing he'd thought to announce himself more safely. She was hurting because of him and he couldn't stand it. He'd give anything to be able to heal her as she had him.

"It's all right," she said breathlessly. She nodded at the half-full cups. "You drink yours. I'll get to mine in a minute, if I get time."

"What's the hurry?" Luce asked, slurping the steaming liquid. He hadn't had a cup of tea in centuries until arriving at Mel's place and now it seemed perfectly natural to drink several a day. He wondered if there was anything she couldn't persuade him to do.

"Raphael called. He said he can get permission for you to enter Heaven again, but you'll have to go through judgement, like any mortal. I said it was ridiculous and I fully intend to argue your case in person. Raphael evidently didn't make it clear..." For the first time, Mel looked annoyed. No, like an angel filled with righteous anger, or at least indignation. He pitied whoever she'd be arguing with; they hadn't a hope in Hell against her.

"Are you sure it's worth the trouble?" he asked. "I mean, it's been so long, I barely remember what it's like up there. It's not like I need to go in — the place is full of righteous angels, being sickeningly kind to each other with no idea of the reality down here. You know I have no patience for them, with their snowy-white reputations and ideals. I don't belong there."

"I'm one of them and so are you. You have every right to be there, just like they do. I have the same ideals, Luce, and you seem to like me just fine," Mel said through gritted teeth as she shut off the tap, shaking her fingers dry in the sink.

Now he felt bad. She seemed so different to all the other angels he knew. None of them knew the conditions down here as well as she did. Delusional, living in their cloudy paradise...they'd never believe her, unless they saw him bleed for themselves. He'd spill his lifeblood for Mel, but not a drop for any of them, he swore. And they'd turn on her like they'd turned on him all those centuries ago. For doing what was necessary – stating the truth.

"I'm coming with you," he announced.

She shook her head. "No, Luce. They'd...react differently to you. I'll go on my own and smooth the way for you. It's better this way."

He snorted. "You expect me to sit here, like some damsel in distress, while you fight my battles for me? Why don't I just wear one of your dresses and you can call me Lucia, too? Even then you'd have to chain me up here to keep me from coming with you. Oh Hell, that brings back memories..." He couldn't help laughing.

"What memories? Do you have a torture room with chains somewhere that you haven't showed me yet?" Mel asked. "Or did you just forget about it until now?"

Luce did his best to regain control of

himself. "No, not any more. I did have a fun couple of decades as Madam Lucia, though, and we had a couple in the Lair. The things those girls could do..."

Mel's face turned blank, almost deliberately, Luce decided. "You worked as a brothel madam? Why doesn't that surprise me? I bet you could've filled up Hell with the people in your whorehouse..."

Luce sobered. "The customers, yes, but most of the girls were absolute saints. The things they put up with from the clients, the pay, the conditions...actually, I never saw their souls again, once they left my employ. Of course, there were a few...the ones who thought it was a fun idea to rob the customers and leave them in an alley somewhere, sometimes still breathing...well, Hell always needs a few more demons."

"You...I'm sorry, Luce, I'm just trying to imagine you in a dress, let alone running a brothel..." Mel shook her head, as if trying to shake the image out of her ears.

Luce tried to smother his grin. "You know, I could show you," he offered eagerly. "There was a lot of leather involved, but I believe some of my favourite designs are still in vogue in modern adult shops. I think they'd suit you better than they ever did me, though."

"Luce." Mel's piercing gaze brought him out of his fantasy. "We weren't discussing your fetish for leather. We were discussing how you should stay here while I'm in Heaven, at least for the moment."

He met her eyes without flinching. "The only way you'll get me to stay here while you're fighting on my behalf is with a strong set of restraints – which brings us nicely back to leather." He let his grin break free. "I fight my own battles in person, Mel. Later, we can celebrate with leather, if you like."

Her expression was priceless and he couldn't help laughing.

# Thirteen

"Please stay here and wait for me," Mel said as she slipped her shoes on. "You won't help your case any by pleading it personally, I swear."

"What are you so worried about? That I'll upset someone? Those angels should learn to take themselves less seriously if just the sight of me offends them," Luce grumbled.

"Angels have long memories, Luce, and you...many of them still blame you for the fall of their loved ones – the angels who followed you and fell with you," Mel said gently.

Luce stopped dead, ignoring his half-laced shoe. "No one fell with me. I fell alone, Mel, and I was left where I landed, shattered. It was dark and cold and hurt like Hell and there was no one to help me. The other angels were banished for what they chose to do, but by the time any of them found me, I'd recovered sufficiently that I didn't need their help. Every one of them made their own decision and I won't be held responsible for their choices and actions!" For a dark moment, he was lost in his past pain in the very depths of a private part of Hell.

Mel's soft kiss to his cheek pulled him out of the Pit, her arms holding him firmly in the present. "Show me," she whispered.

It was as if the ground had dropped away beneath him. Falling through stone and darkness until agony engulfed him and the shadows closed in, but the sensation was dulled, somehow. Maybe it was Mel's embrace, still secure and strong. Blindly, he groped for her in the dark and his lips found hers. He couldn't kiss her hard enough to banish the memories, but they began to fade all the same as she returned his kisses. He tasted salt – oh God, was he crying again? What in Hell would Mel think of him? His eyes jerked open to find out.

Tears cascaded down her face from eyes brimming with sympathy. Not his tears – hers. For him. More precious than any he'd seen before, let alone tasted. "I'm sorry, Luce. I didn't know – and I can barely imagine what it was like to go through it alone." Her sweet, salty kiss was a balm to his slowly healing soul.

"I don't trust your heavenly hosts one little bit. You shouldn't go alone, not to speak on my behalf. I won't let them hurt you like they did me. Let them judge me – they're no better than I am." He regretted the bitterness in his tone, but it was there all the same.

"Luce...please. You're right – any form of judgement is unnecessary and that's exactly what I need to explain. If you come with me, if they judge you today..." She swallowed, as if she wanted to choke down her own words before she spoke them aloud. "I see only darkness. The future is not clear."

Luce grasped her shoulders and looked deep into her eyes, but she turned away to hide her soul. "What aren't you telling me? Mel..."

Closing her eyes, she breathed deeply. "What I swore I wouldn't say. Don't ask me to lie, Luce, for I won't. Please, take my word and trust my advice – that it is a bad idea for you to accompany me to Heaven today. For once, swallow your pride and accept help when it's offered." When her eyes opened, they shimmered with tears. Clouds threatening rain.

If she cried at the mere memories of his fall, there was no way he'd stand by and let them throw her out on his behalf. Luce cemented his resolve. "I'm not sitting here on my arse while you plead for my soul. I intend to be where I belong – by your side. They can judge me to my face."

"I still think it's a bad idea, Luce," she conceded reluctantly. "You should wait."

He shrugged. "If they won't let me in, then I'll sit on the kerb outside the gates, drinking out of a bottle in a brown paper bag, until you reappear." His fingers twitched and the bag appeared in his hand, crumpled around the bottle's metal cap. "And I won't share my single malt with anyone but you."

She laughed and shook her head. Luce wished she'd look less sad, as if she was more worried than she was willing to say. So much for a triumphant entry into Heaven after all these centuries. "To the gates?" he suggested, taking her hand.

She squeezed his fingers strongly. "Yes. With you tagging along, I'll have to do things the old-fashioned way and use the gate."

Together, they translocated to where they could just see the gates. Bathed in misty cloud, the bars shone like pearl in the bright sunlight. Luce felt his dread build as he approached the portal that had kept him out for millennia. Before his eyes, they changed from the happy vision to one that better fitted his mood. Cold iron, brick and desolation, rising from ashen snow.

"The gates of Auschwitz? Luce, that's really not funny," Mel murmured.

Luce left them looking dark. They matched the foreboding he felt as he tightened his grip on Mel's hand. They were going to separate him from Mel, he was sure of it. Let them try. He'd fight with every speck of his spirit, like nothing they'd ever seen.

He focussed on the crunch of snow underfoot. If he stared at his feet, he wouldn't see the looming gates he knew would always keep him out.

"Halt!" a male voice commanded.

Luce looked at the angel on gate duty. A bloke in a white dress, no less. No wonder he looked nervous. He had his wings out, poised for flight, as if he thought it made him look more angelic, instead of like a giant seagull.

Mel gave a little sigh and he felt the softness of her wings making their presence known. She gave him a radiant smile and he was reminded of their first kiss, the night she'd changed him.

"Should I?" he whispered.

Mel nodded encouragingly. Luce breathed deeply. He'd never shown her his dark wings — in fact, few people had seen them. He'd lost count of the number of times he'd lost feathers to the rough rocks in the narrow tunnels. The smell of singed feathers had plagued him so much in Hell that he'd given up showing them altogether centuries ago. Feeling more nervous than ever, he envisioned the vulture he always thought he looked like. The weight on his shoulders told him they were visible. He stretched, feeling the power in his wings for the first time in too long.

"Impressive wingspan," Mel whispered with a wicked smile. Her fingers caressed the leading edge of ebony feathers, making him wish he'd broken his wings out earlier.

Every bit of his being was telling him to enfold her in his arms and fly away with her. He dismissed the silly sensation and folded his wings instead, turning his steady gaze on the now-even-more-nervous angel.

"You need to get in line like everyone else. You'll be called when it's your turn for judgement." The angel pointed a shaky finger toward the long line of white benches, which were occupied by a diverse array of people.

"Sure," Mel replied, tugging at Luce's arm as she led the way to the first empty patch of white wood. As they passed, he noticed people staring and whispering, but none would meet his eyes.

She settled her wings behind her with a shrug of her shoulders and Luce did the same. Looking up at all the people before them, he realised that the only black in the sea of people was what he was wearing – his suit and his wings. The one place in the universe where black didn't let him blend into the background.

He sighed and wished for the first time that he was invisible. This was going to be a long wait.

# Fourteen

"So you're the one who redeemed a demon! Everyone's talking about it," the angel sitting beside Mel gushed. "I didn't think it was possible!" She stared avidly at Luce. "I'm Therese, by the way."

Mel introduced herself, offering the girl her hand. "How long have you been an escort?"

Luce choked with laughter and tried to hide it with a coughing fit. An angel escort?

Therese's eyes shone. "Only a few weeks, I think – it's difficult to tell, with no concept of time up here. This one will be the tenth soul I've escorted to Heaven," she said proudly, gesturing at the girl on her other side.

The teenager stared into space, much like the corpse she probably hadn't left behind very long ago, judging by the modern cut of her clothes.

"You've been around a lot longer, I'm sure. I've heard it takes at least a century before we get wings and yours look so majestic..." Therese added.

Mel smiled modestly at her feet. "Thank you, I have. I've rarely seen the gates this busy, though. What's happened?"

"I heard there was a typhoon in the Pacific, but weekends are always busy lately," Therese said, her expression turning sad.

"Why weekends?"

"Teenagers killed in car accidents, like this one," Therese said softly, nodding at the girl beside her. "The driver, and the passenger who gave him the tequila, were sent elsewhere, but this one was in the back seat when the car hit a tree. None of them were wearing seatbelts. It's like teenage kids think they're indestructible."

Mel smiled sadly. "That hasn't changed. They've been doing that since the first humans – though baiting a rhino or a mammoth with nothing but a pointy stick is perhaps safer than racing in a Ford V8."

Therese's eyes widened. "You've been around that long? Since...since cave people? Is that why you were sent to escort the demon here?"

Mel's smile widened. "No, I volunteered for this one." Luce felt her fingers weave between his, still hot from her scalding this morning. Once again, Luce wished he could heal the damage he'd caused.

Therese lowered her voice, as if she thought her whisper wouldn't carry to Luce's ears. "Where did you find him? I mean, I've never heard of a redeemed demon before..."

"Lucifer's office in HELL."

Therese gasped. "The depths of Hell? But he looks too attractive to be a demon. I heard they had horns, tails, hooves, red skin and things. That one...well, I think I'd volunteer to escort him places, too." She blushed.

"Would you like me to strip and show you

the whole package?" Luce offered, turning to face the angel. "I mean, if you want to admire me as a fine piece of meat, I'd hate for you to miss anything."

She turned redder still. "Are you sure he's redeemed? He doesn't sound it. Shouldn't someone lock him up or something, until they're sure?"

Luce crossed his wrists and lifted them. "Mel can handcuff me to the bed any time she likes and test me until she's satisfied." He realised he still had a pair of cuffs in his jacket pocket, which spurred him to turn on the full force of his wicked grin. "Any beds in Heaven?"

"Shh. Later, perhaps," Mel whispered.

"I didn't think there were submissive demons. I thought they were all arrogant and into whips and chains and things..." Therese's eyes widened. "If you found him in Lucifer's lair, he must be the devil's lover. What will you do when Lucifer comes looking for you?" The little angel looked terrified.

Let him in and give him a cup of tea after letting him use her shower, Luce thought.

"I'm sure I'll manage," Mel replied, looking like she was trying not to laugh.

Luce was struggling, too. The fresh-faced angel without wings had no idea who he was, despite his dark wings. "Mel's definitely a match for Lucifer, any day of the week," he managed to say. A perfect, sublime match, he thought as he glanced at Mel's shapely legs below her skirt.

"Oh, no – they say no angel is, which is why they banished him to Hell. I'm sure I'd be terrified if I so much as saw him," Therese squeaked in fright. "Imagine all the terrible things he could do to you! They say he can corrupt you with just a word or even a look!"

Luce gave her his friendliest smile. "Then it's a good thing I'm on my best behaviour today."

Therese stared at Luce in terror as she realised who he was. "God help me," she murmured.

"Next!" called the gate angel.

Therese looked to be deep in prayer and the line before her had vanished.

"You're up, Therese," Mel said, nudging the

girl. "It was lovely meeting you."

"And...and you," the young angel stammered, pulling the teenage girl's saved soul after her as she hurried to the gate angel's podium.

"You didn't need to scare the poor girl, Luce," Mel said.

"I was just trying to be friendly," he protested. Under her knowing gaze, he relented. "Oh, okay. I've been tempting innocent morsels like her for millennia. Old habits die hard. It's not like I was going to..." He drifted off, not actually sure what he'd have done to the little angel if he'd had her. He stuck his hands in his pockets and scuffed at the snow with his shoes. His fingers closed around the white leather cuffs in his pocket and he brightened. "You know, I meant it about the handcuffs. Any time you think I might be reverting to my old ways, feel free to chain me to the bed. I always keep a spare pair in my pocket, just in case." He started to pull them out so he could show her.

"Shh, put them away, Luce. You'll give everyone the wrong impression. C'mon, it's our turn." She stood and strode toward the gates.

Luce followed her along the row of now-empty benches to what he hoped was his final judgement.

# Fifteen

The dude in the dress swallowed and loosened his collar a little. "N-n-name?" he managed to say.

Mel's mellifluous voice rang out before Luce could open his mouth. "Allow me to present the redeemed angel, Lucifer, Light of the Morning, for re-entry into Heaven."

"L-L-Lucifer?" the saint squeaked. "Does he...does he submit to judgement?"

Luce wanted to ask for an angel who could enunciate properly, but he held his tongue. He didn't want to embarrass Mel. "He does," he said instead.

The man riffled through the pages of his book. Luce stood patiently, waiting.

"You hereby express your contrition for the following sins. Pride, the war against Heaven, the subversive activities of the HELL Corporation, seduction and corruption of one hundred and fifty three thousand, five hundred and sixteen angels..."

Luce tuned out a little at this point, feeling his face flush as he looked everywhere but at Mel. He'd lost count after the first dozen or so. That was millennia ago and they did add up, but he hadn't realised that there were quite that many. A thousand or two, maybe, but surely not a hundred thousand...

"Is that how much practice it took to get as good as you are? No wonder you're the best I've ever had," Mel murmured.

Luce stared at her in surprise and found himself lost in her smile. She was an angel in every sense of the word. "I didn't sleep with all of them," he confessed, then added virtuously, "Some of the men said I wasn't their type."

The angel cleared his throat before continuing, "Impersonation of the Virgin Mary in a strip club on five occasions, salacious thoughts about Melody Angel..."

The strip clubs had been funny. The first time, he'd seen grown men crying and some even praying. A bunch had hurried home to their wives. It was like watching a hilarious movie for the second time — he'd just had to do it again. As for the thoughts about Mel...ah, those were nothing compared to the reality. Maybe he should mention some of his early fantasies to her, just in case she was interested.

"...and the violent rape of Persephone."

The WHAT?

# Sixteen

"I never touched Persephone, the little devil!" Luce protested.

The gate guard seemed to grow in stature, as if he enjoyed being argued with. "Says here the last sin you committed was the violent rape of Persephone, the half-angel who worked as your personal assistant. You left her tied to your bed, bleeding."

"She's lying! I swear I never touched her!" Luce replied hotly. He hadn't. She'd cuffed herself to the bed. If she'd managed to cut herself or rub her wrists raw while trying to get out of the cuffs herself, it wasn't his fault.

"So you don't repent of your final sin?" the guard prompted, the pen shaking in his hand with apparent eagerness.

"I can't repent for something I didn't do. Aren't you supposed to be omniscient? Or the book is, anyway? Check again," Luce insisted. He felt his dread build. He'd given Persephone everything – the powers, the authority, all that came with the darkness in his soul. Did that also mean she had his capacity for deception – that she could accuse him of rape he'd never committed and manage to get it written into the Book of Judgement? He wished he'd killed her instead. Maybe he should have done what they said he had.

"It says here..."

"I vouch for him," Mel interrupted, her voice ringing out across the snow as she strode toward him. She tapped the book with her finger. "He was with me that evening, not Persephone. I spoke to her while he was in my house and she was both uninjured and not restrained in any way. After that phone call, I kept him occupied until I left him in no state to do anything to Persephone that night...or the next morning."

It was the guard's turn to blush. He evidently wasn't used to forthright angels – or perhaps not female ones. Luce grinned. He wondered how much hotter that blush would get if he knew precisely how Mel had kept him occupied.

A woman stormed through the gate toward Luce. "I swear by all I and my daughter hold holy: that demon seduced my daughter, tied her to a bed and raped her when she wouldn't submit to him!" she screeched. "He's not redeemed – he's the demon who's seduced more angels than any other. I'll swear to his guilt. You can't let him in unless he does proper penance for what he did to my daughter!" The gates clanged shut behind her, vibrating a little with the force of the closure.

Luce had never seen her before in his life, though she did bear a passing resemblance to Persephone. Idly, he wondered if the girl's mother knew about her tattoo – or whether the mother had one, too. She looked far too youthful to be Persephone's mother, but appearances were deceiving in Heaven. He'd spent too long in Hell – he wasn't used to souls choosing their age. In Hell, they looked their worst, on principle.

"Why doesn't your daughter speak for herself, Cousin Demeter?" Mel asked reasonably.

Demeter pointed a shaking finger at Luce. "She doesn't trust him not to do it again. Even the thought of him scares her!" Her mouth set in a grim line. "He left my poor girl to take care of his company, doing his job, while he cavorts with another angel, no doubt trying to corrupt her, too! He has no remorse!"

Luce swallowed. "I have no remorse for Persephone. She said if I gave her everything – my company, my power, all of it – she'd tell me how I could find Mel. She took it willingly. All she gave me in return was an address, a phone number and her word they were Mel's. I'd do it again – with less hesitation." Mel's fingers tightened around his. He couldn't look at her. She'd let him into her house and her life. He couldn't remember joy like she'd brought him. She didn't deserve a demoted demon – she deserved an angel of equal rank. He'd do whatever it took to achieve that again – even if it meant surviving this inquisition. He took a deep breath. "I'm sorry if anything I've done caused Persephone pain or grief. That was never my intention." He gritted his teeth.

"So...so you do repent all of your crimes?" the gate guard cried in relief, sweat trickling down his cheek. Luce realised he wasn't the only one under pressure in this interrogation. The gates slowly started to swing open. "In that case, I can permit you entry into..."

"NO!" boomed a new voice. "I haven't stood guard for countless centuries against him and his kind, only to let a demon in now. I banished him to Hell as he deserved. Demons cannot be redeemed. I won't stand by and permit the most damned demon of them all to sneak into Heaven on an angel's skirts." An armoured angel stepped in front of the gates, lifting a sword that burst into flame. "You shall not pass!"

Oh Hell. He had to pop up, just when everything seemed to be going so well. If he had a nemesis, it was Michael. Mel was no match for that flaming sword.

Mel burst out laughing. "You've been watching too many movies, Michael. Even I've seen that one. As for my skirt..." She shimmied out of the garment, letting it puddle in the snow at her feet for a moment, before reaching down to retrieve it. Flashing her white cotton undies in the process, she ignored Luce's wide grin, the gate guard's blush and Michael's attempt to turn his head away. "If I remember correctly, Michael, you were just as eager as Luce to get into my skirts. Here!" She balled up the white skirt and lobbed it at the armoured angel.

Awkwardly, he batted it away with the sword, setting the skirt alight as it tumbled to his feet. He did a clumsy, clanking jig on the spot to put out the flames. The resulting black scorch marks up his legs spoiled the shiny armour. Luce smothered a laugh as Michael ripped the metal helmet off his head. Red-faced, he demanded, "What are you laughing at, demon?"

"Well, I can certainly see why the lady

prefers me," Luce drawled.

"All the more reason to keep you and your kind out!" declared Michael. "You deserve an eternity in Hell for corrupting just one angel, let alone a hundred thousand, five hundred and..."

"A hundred and fifty three thousand, five hundred and sixteen," the gate guard corrected.

Michael stared at him in panic. "A hundred and fifty three thousand..."

"Five hundred and sixteen," the guard repeated, with some satisfaction.

"Look, I've said I'm sorry for any wrong I've done. But there's more to it. Every one of those angels was a willing participant," Luce said. "And after seeing you two, I'm not surprised. Skirts and dresses and metal – haven't you seen what men wear on Earth these days?"

"I'll send you right back to the Pit before you can make it five hundred and seventeen with Mel!" Michael shouted, waving the sword so the flames streaked through the air. Demeter stood with her arms crossed, nodding. She still kept her distance from

Michael, her eyes firmly fixed on the erratic sword. "You're only using her to get back into Heaven so you can try to take over again!"

Luce turned to Mel. "I swear that's not true. If this weren't your home, I wouldn't want to set foot in there ever again. Mel, please believe me. I might've fantasised about corrupting you before, but now that I know you, I couldn't. You can see into my heart" – he thumped his chest – "and into my soul. You know I wouldn't do that to you, don't you?"

Mel nodded serenely, her eyes intent on Luce's. "I know exactly what you would and wouldn't do," she said.

Luce felt a chill sweep across his heart. Did she know him better than he knew himself? Had she brought him here, only to betray him so Michael could banish him more permanently to the Pit?

No, she wouldn't do that. She was too kind for that – and she'd tried to dissuade him from coming with her. Surely she wouldn't...she was the only one who believed in him, that he could be redeemed. His hope was all hers.

"You may have her convinced, but never

me. I will not let you pass into Heaven!" Michael shouted, lowering the sword like a parking barrier across the gate.

"What about my daughter? What reparation will he make for what he did to her?" Demeter growled, looking from the gate guard to Michael.

Both men shrugged. "He said he was sorry..." the guard ventured.

"The Hell he's sorry!" she shouted. Her eyes glowed with fury. "I'll send him back to the Pit myself."

She pulled Michael's sword from his steel grip. The blade flared up, giving her eyes a ruddy glow, as she held it like a cricketer about to hit a ball for six. She charged forward, her eyes fixed on Luce.

No one seemed able to move.

Luce recovered first, summoning his traditional bident to block the blow he could see angling toward him. He wouldn't let that blade blast him to Hell against his will again. That was one blow to the balls he wouldn't take.

Mel recovered second, moving between

Demeter and Luce. Her resonant "NO!" was enough to freeze Luce.

Faced with a righteous angel, Demeter faltered and the flame fizzled. She dropped the sword, but it was too late.

Luce tried to lower his weapon, too, but both barbs had already pierced Mel. The bident had passed right through her chest, the red-glazed prongs protruding from her white shirt.

"No," Luce moaned. "Mel..." He dismissed his weapon back to the depths of Hell, so it wouldn't do any further damage to Mel's body. His eyes fixed on the fading bronze fork until it had disappeared altogether.

He pulled her against him, trying to let her down gently onto the snow, which now felt incredibly cold and hard. Beneath his knees, the snow turned to cloud – much softer and warmer for Mel, he realised distantly.

Blood blossomed over Mel's breasts, like obscene flowers on a corpse. There were tears in her eyes.

Luce didn't care who was watching him. He kissed Mel's lips and tasted the salt of her blood. A nagging thought crossed his mind that angels couldn't be killed, but Michael's sword and his own fork weren't normal weapons — they were imbued with more power than anything else he'd encountered. He'd been banished from Heaven by one of them...and she'd been touched by both.

Mel didn't deserve his fate.

"Hold on, my love. Everything will be as it should be. You'll see." She smiled and a bubble of blood appeared at the corner of her lips.

"You'll be all right," he said, praying for it to be true. "Just lie still, Mel, and someone will heal you.""

If he were the angel he once was, he could have healed her at a touch. Instead, he was forced to beg for help from the angels who'd condemned him. "What are you staring at?" he shouted. "Someone help her. Help her!"

No one moved.

The light in Mel's eyes started to fade. With what looked like great effort, she swallowed. "I love you," she whispered. She looked at him one last time and her eyes closed.

Luce couldn't take his eyes off her. He

thought it was his sight blurring, as sunlight tinted his tears of grief to gold. The body in his arms became lighter, though, so that he couldn't help but notice. Her skin was turning to gold, dissolving into a fine mist. The mist curled upward, forming a cloud above his head. The bloodstained shirt in his hands fell limp with no body to fill it.

The cloud roiled, streaming like cirrus in a high wind, then faded into nothing. She was gone.

He crumpled the shirt in his arms, still warm from Mel's body and smelling of her perfume. Actually, it was lumpy with her underwire bra, so he folded it carefully so as not to show her underwear to anyone. He looked around for her knickers and scooped them up, too, hiding them inside her shirt. He didn't trust Michael with them — not that he trusted Michael at all, self-righteous bastard.

Luce felt his fury build. Mel was his everything and they'd taken her away from him by standing there doing nothing. "You killed her," he accused Demeter, before shifting his glare to Michael. If Michael hadn't brought his infernal sword and barred their way...if Demeter hadn't snatched it from him to attack Luce...if Mel hadn't felt he needed to be protected... "She didn't deserve to die!"

"No," the gate guard piped up, looking scared, "you did. It's right here in the Book of Judgement. You brought your Hellish weapon here and thrust it through her body."

Luce gasped for breath. He did it. He did it. He'd killed her – the one person he'd ever loved.

"She didn't deserve you, either," Michael said. "You'd only drag her down to Hell and hide her from all those who love and need her."

I love her, Luce thought. No, I loved her. For she's forever gone to me, whether she lives or not. If she ever sees me again, her eyes will accuse and condemn. For I killed her. I killed her.

"Some things can't be redeemed," he muttered. "Now I know what it is to be damned."

Shadows swirled, summoned back to his dark soul. There was no light for him, not any more. Perhaps there never was. He belonged in Hell.

# Seventeen

"You will never know the domination of Earth or Heaven. Your realm will be Hell and the boundaries of your rule. For your advisors, take the angels who fought for you, for they, too, will fall from Heaven, never to return. GO!" Michael waved his sword and the flames seemed to blaze higher than the angel behind them.

Luce could feel fear in the archangel, but the sword Michael wielded was more powerful than any other weapon the worlds had known.

Nevertheless, Luce knew he was right. "Those beings aren't perfect and they never will be. They will destroy all we've created here. They are few now, but they will outnumber us in time and, when that happens, they will stop listening. What will you do with them when they are not fit for Heaven or Earth any more?"

"Why, we'll send them to you, to Hell. You and yours can punish them as you wish, as a deterrent to the rest. They can join you in permanent exile," Michael announced. The angels who followed him laughed.

"What will you do when Hell is full?" Luce asked.

"It won't be full until this world is ended. Then, we will speak again," Michael said, drawing back his sword.

"Take your best shot," Luce growled, opening his arms wide. He wouldn't show fear or weakness, though he knew the other angel had won. Even exiled to Hell, he wouldn't acknowledge defeat. "And do not miss, for if I see you again, be assured that I will kill you."

The burning blade drove deep into his chest

before he could close his mouth.

The pain was blinding, sending him to his knees. Luce struggled to speak, but Michael gave him no opportunity. He ripped the sword, now dripping with blood, from Luce's body. If Luce thought the pain from the entry wound was bad, he wasn't prepared for the agony of the exit. His vision went dark.

"Fall, demon. You have no dominion here or on Earth. No one will help you now."

Luce felt his body plummeting through darkness. The cold cling of cloud, the furious rush of wind, weightlessness in his limbs, yet still he fell. His body burned as if cloven in two by the sword before it was torn free, but this became his only feeling as the icy plunge took his sense of touch along with his sight. He heard the air scream past, though he couldn't summon the breath to scream. He could taste his own blood like tar in his throat and wished the torment would end.

His prayer was answered. He hit unyielding rock, pain exploding as his bones shattered from the impact. When the icy air stole his pain, it was a relief.

Only darkness, silence and the cold kiss of stone, sending him into oblivion.

Wonderful. Now he was having flashbacks about his first fall from Heaven. Luce waited impatiently for the memory to fade enough for reality to return.

In the absence of sound, the first thing he became aware of was scent. Coconut and lemon. No, mandarin and neroli. Jasmine, sandalwood, lavender and...myrrh. His lips lifted in a smile. Only Mel smelled like that.

He opened his eyes dreamily, so he could see her as well as smell her, but he lay in darkness. The scent was so clear, though, as if she was right there with him. He lifted his nose, trying to work out where she was, and felt the touch of cotton on his face.

Mel's ripped shirt.

Luce jerked up, shivering on the cold, stone floor.

Mel. Gone forever – by his hand.

Pain exploded anew, worse than his first crash into Hell.

He'd never see her again.

# Eighteen

"I love you," she'd whispered, even as she'd died at his hands. What kind of tragedy ended with words of love for her murderer from his victim? Who would write such a fate for anyone?

William Shakespeare. *Othello.*

Luce wondered if there was a circle in Hell reserved for authors who killed their characters in stupid circumstances, as he'd killed Mel. Or maybe just the bitches who tortured their heroes, subjecting them to the sort of pain gnawing at his heart now. If there wasn't, he was going to create one, with boiling pools of ink...or pages that delivered countless paper cuts...or computers that only had dodgy touchscreens with terrible autocorrect...

Mel was no Desdemona. She wouldn't have let him wallow in his misery or any other feeling. She'd have insisted on a shower, a change of clothes and some tea. Yes, he was damned, but he was the Lord of Hell. He'd damn well make sure the other damned souls regretted their crimes as much as he did his. Killing his beloved angel...

He climbed laboriously to his feet. Balled up in his hand were the remains of her clothes. He buried his nose in the bloodstained shirt, wanting to catch a whiff of her perfume. Neroli, jasmine and myrrh. Oh God, Mel...

He spread her clothes out on his desk. The pierced shirt. The white, lace-edged bra... that had holes in it, too. Only her knickers were intact. They were all he had of her – the last clothes she'd worn, stained with her lifeblood and marked with her scent. He'd treasure them until the world ended. He folded the underwear carefully inside the shirt and placed the whole bundle in his desk drawer. It wouldn't do to show his weakness to the lesser demons of his realm. What would she have wanted him to do if he lost her?

She'd want him wearing a clean shirt. The one he wore to dinner with her in the office, the night she'd first kissed his cheek. He summoned the item with a thought, stripping out of his soiled clothes.

Fresh shirt, then fresh pants, underwear and socks. Tie. Hair brushed, face washed and shaved. Teeth sparkling. He was dealing with demons and damned souls. None of them deserved to know about the hole in his heart, the place reserved for her.

He turned the climate control thermostat down, hoping it would help him maintain his icy calm. Just the way Mel had in negotiations with anyone, angel or demon.

I love you, too, Mel, he thought. Like no one else before or since. If the remainder of his existence was to be a living Hell, at least he'd be in the right place for it. No one else would notice the difference.

# Nineteen

Mel felt her body slowly coalesce. No one had told her just how much it would hurt to be stabbed and then disintegrate. Raphael owed her big time for this; as did Michael. She couldn't recall ever being this furious, but she'd never heard of an angel offering false judgement before. They'd have Hell to pay on this one – and that was after she was done with them. Heaven wasn't happy with them, either.

When she could feel her fingers moving, she

dared to open her eyes. She took stock of her surroundings before moving from her crouch. "Where's Luce?" she asked. "More importantly, where are my clothes? Little brother, if you think hiding my clothes is funny..."

Michael's metal-clad foot nudged the small pile of ash. "Well, this was your skirt. Why'd you tell him I used to dress up in your clothes when I was a kid? He'll think I'm..."

"He doesn't know you're my little brother. I'm sure Luce didn't...where is he? I thought you said you'd wait for me to return before you opened the gates for him." She stretched as she stood up, feeling the flex of her muscles in her rebuilt body. "And where did he get that fork from?"

"We think he summoned it from Hell. He can't have given up everything – he must still be the Lord of Hell. That makes him very dangerous," Peter piped up.

Mel dismissed the danger. "He gave up everything he owned – all the power he had – to Persephone. His dominion over Hell is a sacred trust – he can't give that up. It's part of who he is. I saw him use that power in my house and again when he brought that weapon here from Hell. Angel or demon, Luce is still the Lord of Hell – and, ultimately, the leader of every demon there is. I need to know where he is."

Michael cleared his throat, turning his back on Mel. "He vanished, just after you did. We think he banished himself back to Hell permanently."

Peter took the cloth from beneath his book and tossed it to Mel, who began wrapping it around herself like a sarong. As he set the book down again, a loose sheet of paper slipped out into the cloud at his feet.

"Why?" she asked. "He passed your damn test, with your trumped-up charges on that little memo. I'm sure you're not allowed to add extra pages to the Book of Judgement. Your little unauthorised tribunal. I agreed not to reveal my identity until after you were done, but if I'd known what you were going to do with NO authority whatsoever, I'd never have permitted it. Oh, and if I ever see that sword again, it'll be too soon. I swear I'll have it welded into a city sewer main. Do you know how much that hurt? When I see Raphael, he's going to be in my debt for the next millennium, at least. And someone owes me new clothes and matching underwear. Tell me you at least let Luce know he was free to enter Heaven."

"He disappeared before we could tell him," Michael whispered hoarsely.

"Why didn't you follow him?" Mel demanded.

"He's gone to Hell. We can't follow him there – can't even see him. He's masking himself from us, somehow," Michael replied, a little louder.

"But not from me," Mel said softly. "He carries a part of me with him."

Michael seemed to gain stature. "He has WHAT?" he exploded. "You sold your soul to Lucifer? What happens when he finds out who you are? What possessed you to do something so...so...STUPID?"

Mel turned cold eyes on her brother, feeling all restraint slip away. Standing in her full glory, she saw reflected gold glitter in Michael's fearful eyes. Too little, too late for Luce. Her voice held more power than she intended as she said, "I sold nothing. I gave it freely, for it was my only hope of helping him. He already knows who I am. I thought I could send him home to Hell when his soul repulsed the spirit I breathed into him, but he welcomed me...with love. Our souls bonded and some small spark remains with him – I can sense it still." She reached out to the soul that was so closely connected to her own. "Screened by a thick cloud of darkness, and in the middle is despair. What did you tell him?" She couldn't hide the horror in her voice. She'd never sensed a soul in so much pain before. And a soul who didn't deserve it.

Fear seemed to have stolen Michael's ability to speak. He knew she knew.

"He really thought he'd killed you," Peter said.

"So he condemned himself to Hell? You realise I'm going to have to go in there after him," Mel stated. She struggled with the thick fabric, which wouldn't quite meet. There simply wasn't enough of it.

"You don't have to," Michael ventured. "You could just leave him to his fate. He is the ruler of Hell, after all. He does sort of belong there."

Mel shook her head slowly. "You don't get it, do you? We can't bond with demons or the fallen without falling ourselves, and I am as I ever was. Instead, he changed – for me. He's an angel – the same as us. He doesn't belong there any more than we do. Makes me wonder how many others are there who don't need to be. He's there because of me and I won't let him suffer any more. Enough is enough."

"But, Mel, no angel who's ever made it out of there has remained, well, an angel," Michael hedged. "Most never leave. Don't go – it's too great a risk, to lose you for a demon you think might have changed." Far from a command, he sounded like he was begging. "Please, Mel..."

"Are you volunteering to go in my place?" Mel asked. "Someone has to set this right."

Michael shook his head violently. "Please. I only did it to protect you. I couldn't...I wouldn't...and he'd never listen to me. Let alone forgive..."

"Nothing can justify what you did to him. If my fate is to enter Hell, then I will follow it. And let you live with the knowledge that it's your fault. You won't stop me, Michael."

He dropped to his knees and grabbed her hand, his eyes entreating. "Mel, don't. No angel can survive Hell without being tainted. Just look at him..."

"Show me." Mel looked at Michael's face and deeper, too – to the very depths of his soul. She saw an angel forcing another to fall into Hell...for her. Somehow, that angel had emerged as the demon she'd met on the day of her interview. She snapped, "You're suggesting I should leave a redeemed man in Hell because it's too hard and you're too scared to do it yourself? After what you did to him? There's a reason you're standing guard on the gate, little brother, while I've been guiding the governments of the world for centuries. No one else has ever redeemed a demon – until me. You three just sent an innocent man to Hell without a word of protest. And I know this isn't the first time." Mel stared at Demeter and the two men until they found the cloud beneath their feet fascinating. "Michael and Peter, you agree that he passed your test – and you won't cause any further trouble to prevent him from entering Heaven?"

Both men nodded.

"Yes, Lady Muriel," Peter managed to say, backed up by Michael's scared silence.

"Demeter, he never touched Persi, though she offered herself to him. I watched over her myself – I was worried about the outcome, too, yet events spun out as he said." Mel kept her gaze on Persephone's mother.

Demeter bowed her head. "I believe you, Lady Muriel. Persi never said what he'd done – simply that he left her naked and hurt in his home. I didn't realise all he hurt was her pride. You do understand why I had to see for myself, if he really could be redeemed, as you say." She swallowed. "I'm sorry I burned your shirt. I wish you luck. A redeemed demon...gives us hope of redemption for the others."

Mel took a deep breath and released it, feeling the strength in her newly formed body.

She'd need it in Hell. "I'll see you all on my return and Heaven won't help you if you stand in my way again. From HELL Corporation to the Pit itself. Now, more than ever, it's time for me to go to Hell."

With barely a gold shimmer in the air, she was gone. The tiny tablecloth fluttered in the firmament, buoyed by the breeze of her passage.

"What do we do now?" Peter asked Michael.

"Pray," Michael replied. "I'd prefer to let a hundred demons into Heaven with my blessing than agree to let Mel go to Hell."

"Why did you let her go, then?" Peter persisted.

Michael's laughter was hollow. "Nothing can stop Lady Muriel from fulfilling her destiny. Not you, not me, not Raphael. Not even all the forces of Heaven combined."

"What about the forces of Hell?"

Michael closed his eyes in defeat. "We're about to find out, aren't we?"

# Twenty

Much like Luce's inability to enter Heaven without passing through the gates, Mel knew she couldn't translocate herself directly into Hell. There were protocols to be observed. Instead, she placed herself in the desert sand a short distance from the entrance, in full view of the cave mouth. She'd expected a fiery portal, like the stories said, but she'd take this cold, rocky alternative if it meant she wouldn't singe her wing feathers on the way in. She did have to keep up appearances, after all.

She reached out once more for Luce, sensing his despairing soul amid a collective moan of so many others. So much pain, concentrated in one place. That was Hell. She couldn't understand how any angel could want to stay here. She could feel tears forming in her eyes already and she wasn't even inside.

She passed between jagged rocks, wondering how many souls it would take to wear them smooth. She knew it was a matter of perspective – she saw Hell this way, while others saw the inferno, their worst nightmares, or, in Luce's case, perhaps a friendly welcome mat. No, surely not even he saw that.

The imps had told her that Hell was as much a place of perception as Heaven – perhaps this place had inspired post-modernist thinkers to formulate their theories on perspectives and reality. She smothered laughter as she stepped into the darkness, letting her body glow just a little so she could see clearly. If she'd known the fires of Hell would be extinguished for her visit, she'd have brought a torch.

Now it was only a matter of time before her

natural radiance brought her to the attention of some of Hell's darker denizens; demons and souls who had inhabited the place for so long that they were unrecognisable for the angels and humans they once were. She shrugged. The one she searched for was the oldest, darkest and most powerful of them all – and he loved her. Nothing else mattered but finding Luce.

Mel shivered as a cold breeze caught her. She looked down and realised she'd lost the tiny tablecloth somewhere along the way.

A naked angel, taking on all the forces of Hell to claim their leader. Oh, someone up there sure had a sense of humour. So be it. No one could say she'd chosen the easy way, she mused, chuckling quietly. Her laughter seemed an odd sound in this dark place, but no less unusual than her own, glowing self.

"I'm coming for you, Luce," she said, her words ringing out in the darkness. "I've redeemed you once and nothing will stop me from doing the same again. I know your soul."

Only silence greeted her statement, until she swore as she smacked her foot on a rock.

Limping slightly, she strode on. Luce's soul was worth more than a simple stubbed toe.

124

# Twenty-One

The words were carved deep into the stone:

**All hope abandon ye who enter here.**

Mel half expected despair to settle on her like a heavy blanket, but her hopes were higher than ever. Luce was near – she could feel his presence. She had to hope, for not doing so would be to lose Luce to despair and a fate he didn't deserve – something she couldn't do. He'd asked for her help, even if it had taken him millennia to do so.

She'd come so far – she'd drag hope kicking and screaming to the very depths of Hell. She paused to look at the dark letters. She didn't want to deface something that had evidently taken a lot of time and effort to carve, but she wouldn't leave without leaving her own mark on the place. Eternity in the absence of hope had never been her intention.

She concentrated and summoned a short, pine plank. The wood developed a shiny white sheen as Mel's idea took form. Letters appeared in tacky red gloss, cursive suiting it better than the plain Latin letters her sign would cover. She paused and thought for a moment, before adding a spray of red glitter, spread across the sign's surface. Not hiding her smile, she hung the sign above the doorway, so that it concealed the stark letters beneath.

She looked up at her handiwork. "A sexy devil lives here," she read aloud, before starting to laugh. She raised her voice to shout, "Luce, the longer you leave me to my own devices, the more I'll decorate your domain! I hope you like red glitter."

She was answered by silence, but her own amusement was enough. She wanted to see Luce's face when he noticed the sign – and she hoped it would be soon.

# Twenty-Two

The cavern was dim and Mel waited for her eyes to adjust. Her own luminance brightened to compensate – she stood out so much anyway, a little light wouldn't make much difference. She could hear the trickle of water as a stream ran deep into the cave system.

She stumbled over some unevenness on the ground and reached for the nearest rock to steady herself. The rock moaned under her hand and she realised her mistake. The soul that had once been a man was grey and huddled, shaped much like a rock, and his stillness only added to the impression of stone. She let her fingers linger on the man, closing her eyes to see what he did, if only for a moment.

Loud buzzing drew her attention to the cloud of wasps surrounding them. The insects flew in to sting the man, who had his hands over his face instead of trying to brush them away. Mel tried to shoo the cloud from him, but it paid no attention to her. She waved her hands more widely, hoping to give the man some small relief, but the wasps disappeared as she broke contact with the damned soul.

The man endured eternal torment – in his own head, she realised. Tears sprang to her eyes. How could anyone sustain hope when they were tortured by their own imagination? Imps and illusions.

She touched another crouched soul – this one appeared vaguely female. She heard the woman's hoarse screams as maggots crawled through the gaping wounds all over her body. Mel reeled back, letting the woman go, as the wiggling, white larvae vanished from her sight

– though not from her memory.

She looked around. These two souls were not alone – there were thousands of huddled figures in the cavern, stretching out into the darkness. She stifled a sob. This was Hell – this sea of hopelessness. She wasn't surprised that Luce had been so eager to leave. She'd leave now if it weren't for him.

Out of the darkness, she heard an old man's cackling laughter.

"This is no place for you, angel. Go back to where you belong."

Mel proceeded carefully toward the voice, only to stop in surprise. The trickling stream caressed her toes as she stared. Spanning the tiny rivulet was a flat riverboat, sitting like a bridge from one side of the water to the other. A man stood in the bow, his head hooded, a pole suspended from his hand into the shallow water. "Go home to Heaven. Hell is not for your kind, unless you wish to fall."

Mel drew herself up. "I am here for Lucifer and I won't leave until I've spoken with him."

"Then you'll never leave, angel. How will you withstand Hell when even the damned souls in the vestibule can drive you to tears?"

She felt more tears trickle down her cheeks, adding salt to the stream. "This is horrible enough – and it's not even Hell?" She couldn't leave him here. How could she leave any of them?

"No, little angel. Go back to whoever sent you. If the Lord of Hell wishes to see you, he'll find you, and you'll wish he hadn't," he said, sounding kind.

She thought she recognised the voice, though it had been a long time since she'd heard it. "Charon?" she asked.

"Everyone knows I'm the ferryman here, angel. If you're a new escort, so fresh you'd never heard of me before today, you should leave quickly. No angel lasts long here."

"You'll see more clearly if you take your hood off, Charon," Mel said with a smile. "Don't you recognise me?"

Down came the hood. The old man beneath squinted at her, looking puzzled. Some spark of recognition kindled in his eye and his shock showed. "Lady Muriel? What are you doing here?"

"I told you – I'm here for Lucifer," she said sadly.

"No. The risk is too great. You're needed on Earth – among men, where you can make a difference. Here, there is only despair."

"Charon, you know better than to tell a Domination what to do. I will enter Hell and descend to whatever depths your Lord has hidden himself in. He can't hide from me."

"I won't take you across the river, Lady Muriel," the old man said firmly, his hand shaking as his fingers grasped the pole.

Mel laughed as she took another step into the stream. Even in the middle, the water was barely above her ankles, a cleansing coolness between her toes. "I don't need your boat. I can walk across just fine."

His eyes widened in shock once more. "You can see through the illusions? Even the Lord of Hell traverses the River Acheron by boat. Lady Muriel...don't lose yourself in the darkness here. Some of the shadows here are darker than anything on the surface."

She bowed her head in thanks. "I will do my best. If you see Lucifer, tell him I'm looking for him. Remind him that he is in my debt and I will collect."

He bowed in response. "I will, Lady Muriel, and I wish you well. My hopes go with you."

# Twenty-Three

"I never should've bought that round. Buying rounds only ever ends badly. Someone else always orders the most expensive cocktail and you're left to pick up the bill..." a voice slurred. "Should've stuck to drinking mead."

Mel laughed. "Buying rounds is always trouble. I miss mead like we used to get."

She followed the sound of more slurred imprecations and found a man sitting submerged in shallow water. She splashed across to him. "Where was the best mead made?"

"Larissa, in Aeolus. Did you ever taste it?" the man asked dreamily. "I owned the first tavern in Larissa and none could compare to it. They tried to copy my recipes, but making good mead is an art..." The man looked blearily at her. "Do I know you? No one's talked to me in so long. It's like I'm invisible..."

"If you make the best mead in Larissa, then you must be Acheron, Demeter's son. I believe I did taste it once, but that was a long time ago. What happened to you?"

"Bunch of men were all that was left of a huge army. Defeated, they came into my tavern for a drink. Wanted to drown their sorrows before heading home. I poured a round of mead, took their coin, then headed to the cellar for another jug when I heard their story. My shout and all. When I came back up, the crazy general of the winning army was wrecking my tavern. Some idiot named Zeus. Him and his men broke everything. I tried to stop them, but some of them picked me up and dragged me to the river. I woke up in the water and I'm waiting for the dawn, so I can see to walk home. My wife'll be waiting."

Mel understood Demeter's desire for redemption of those here now, seeing her son sitting like a drunkard in the gutter. She hadn't the heart to tell him that his wife and family were long dead, as was he.

"I saw your mother recently. She sends her love," Mel said instead.

"Mother's the one who taught me to make mead," Acheron said happily, stretching out in the water, his hands behind his head. He started to snore.

Mel sighed sadly for Acheron's fate. To everyone else, he was simply a part of the river that bore his name now. She resolved to find some mead when she reached the surface once more, to drink to Acheron's memory.

# Twenty-Four

Mel thought she could see a flicker of light in front of her, wavering as if reflected on water. She strode forward more confidently. Perhaps she'd finally found some of the hellfire she'd heard about. This place seemed far more dank, dark and depressing than the fiery place of torment she'd been led to believe it was. All she felt for the denizens of this place was pity. And Luce – lost among them, somewhere. She could feel his presence still, but she knew he was much deeper than she'd reached thus far.

Her heart ached for him – he seemed so lonely. "I'm here, Luce. You'll see me sooner if you come to me. I'm dependent on your demons for directions." She sensed no change in him, so she doubted he'd heard her words. She ploughed on.

Mel squeezed through a narrow crevice and found the cavern widened considerably after it. It had to, to accommodate the columns stretching as far as she could see. This cave was lit from above, faint moonlight or sunlight shimmering through the dripping water and slick stalactites to reach the pool below. The whole room looked like some sort of castle, with towers and walls made by limestone accretions over many millennia. Even the columns were natural formations, where stalactites and stalagmites, or stalactites and the floor, had met and married.

She hadn't expected to stumble across something so beautiful inside Hell. She wanted to ask Luce about it – what dark secrets did this place hold? Or was this place somewhere he came to for respite from the darkness throughout the rest of Hell? She stepped carefully into the pool to take a closer look at a glimmering column, noticing glow worms for the first time. This cave must have been close to the surface, to capture and keep Earth insects.

Something bumped her foot and she looked down. A blissful-faced man floated on the surface, his eyes wide open and glazed, as if in a drugged stupor. Mel carefully backed away from him, apologising, but he didn't reply. Only now did she notice that the pool was full of such floating figures – all of them drifting upon the surface, staring up.

She left the water completely at this point, not wanting to make contact with any of the other strange souls. Perhaps this was where Hell's denizens were rewarded for good behaviour – or it could be some form of torture she couldn't fathom.

She left them to their pretty play of light on water and limestone. When she found Luce, she could ask him about the place. Hell was stranger than she'd thought – but still sad. Drifting in a dream was not much of an improvement on living in fear of an illusion, as the souls in the vestibule had been.

A soft sound made her look down. A pink bundle of feathers lay at her feet – it looked like it had flown into the cave but had been unable to find the way out. She lifted the bird, feeling the faint vibration of its fast-beating heart. "This is no place for you, little one," she whispered, kissing the cockatoo's back. The bird turned its head to regard her and let out a shriek as it lifted its crest, flashing a sunset spectrum of feathers.

Mel closed her eyes and traced the light to its source in the desert sky above. She breathed on the bird, sharing her knowledge of the way out. "Fly," she said, releasing the Major Mitchell cockatoo. White wings spread, flapped and sent the creature flying upward and away. A final shriek of farewell filtered through the caves in its wake.

She shook her own wings, wishing she could follow the cockatoo from darkness into daylight.

"I'll see you fly out of here, too, Luce! You're going to spread those wings for me, because I love you and I won't leave you here," she shouted.

A pink feather landed by her foot and Mel leaned over to pick it up. Pink fluffiness was as out of place in Hell as she was. Luce should have come to confront her by now. Perhaps she hadn't made her presence clear enough to him yet.

Mel's eyes darted around the cavern, looking for a flat stretch of wall for her canvas. This time, she'd try her hand at cave painting instead of sign writing. Metaphorically speaking.

She heard the cockatoo shriek faintly again, joined by the sound of several more birds. A flock in flight, she decided, in garish pink and red, holding the image of the birds in her head as she summoned the coloured pigments she'd need to bring the image to life. White and pink, red and yellow...Mel opened her eyes to survey her handiwork. Larger than life, the pink cockatoos soared on the limestone, headed up and out. As she would be, as soon as she found Luce.

She'd carry him out in her arms if she had to, like a reclaimed soul for Heaven. For that's what he was. And if there was hope for him, then there was hope for all the others here, too.

# Twenty-Five

The two junior demons shuffled their feet and stared at the stone. Luce knew he'd remember their names if he thought about it long enough, but he didn't want to waste any more time or thought on them. Luce found he grew more impatient the longer they took to get to the point.

"Why haven't there been regular reports on the number of new souls entering the gate?" he demanded.

"We've been working in the office and..."

one mumbled.

"But you've been back a week, without a word between the two of you." Luce looked from one to the other and still couldn't see their eyes. "What's wrong with the gate?"

One of them jerked his head up, his wide, frightened eyes meeting Luce's. "We don't know who did it! Everything was fine – a bit quiet, maybe, after the dangerous drivers came in for the weekend, so we stopped for a smoke..."

"You were smoking on the premises while on duty?" Luce boomed. "You know there are human laws about that sort of thing..."

"We weren't in the office – we went back inside to light up, like we always do. It was raining out," the second demon whined. "There isn't a procedure about smoking in Hell. Just outside and in the office."

Luce took a deep breath. He'd forgotten. It'd been that long since he'd smoked anything, after spending so long in the human world, that it'd completely slipped his mind that it was normal to smoke here. "Go on. The gate?" he prompted.

"Yeah, the gate," the first one continued, glancing at his companion. "Look, it was fine. No one around and no trouble. So we stopped for a break and when we came back, it was there. We didn't see who it was. But there was this stink of angel around..."

"Just the stink – no sign of the angel, though," the second piped up. "We looked around outside – got wet and everything – but couldn't find him anywhere."

Luce grunted impatiently. "Did you think to check inside?"

"What angel would be crazy enough to come into Hell?" The two guard demons looked at each other and laughed.

"Angels do nothing without a reason," Luce said softly. "So if the angel left – what did he do before he left?" He kept his eyes on the squirming guards.

"He defaced the sign, sir! Left a note," Demon Two said helpfully.

"A note." Luce couldn't have made his voice more expressionless if he tried. "And what did this note say?"

The guards exchanged nervous glances.

Demon One coughed. "Best if you see for yourself, Lord Lucifer. You'll probably understand it better than we could."

Luce nodded and stood. On his signal, all three of them transported directly to the cave entrance. The rain had stopped temporarily, but the damp on the ground and in the air, compounded by the heavy cloud above, promised that their reprieve was brief. God, the desert rain smelled good.

One of the demons lit a cigarette with shaking hands, dropping his match in the damp sand. A wisp of smoke writhed up as it extinguished.

A flash of light caught Luce's eye. For a moment, he thought the match had flared up again, but it looked redder than the tiny sulphur flame. He scanned the wet ground. It looked like flecks of metal or glittering stone on the red desert sand. He glanced up at the gate arch.

Red glitter. He scuffed at the flecks in the mud, seeing the colour bleed out, leaving only the silver behind.

Michael. Who else could it be, but the cross-dressing angel who hated him so passionately? Only Michael would be cruel enough to taunt him about the loss that was still raw in his heart – and in such a childish way, like a teenager with a spray can in an alley on Earth.

"If you see any more angels, I want you to subdue them on sight and then bring them to me. We won't tolerate this kind of disrespect. Hell is not a place for jokes," Luce said shortly, trying to hide his pain. He'd give anything to hear Mel call him sexy again. Hell, he'd give anything to hear her laughter at one of his jokes.

"What do you want us to do with the sign, sir?" Demon One asked timorously.

Luce shrugged. "Leave it where it is. It's true." He turned and said, "Remember – any more angels – bring them straight to me, in my office. I don't have time to be traipsing all over Hell because of some silly angel's idea of a prank."

As he shifted from the gate to his desk in the depths, he caught one guard whispering to the other, "So which demon is the sign talking about?"

He wanted to turn and shout at his subordinates, if only to release some of his anger and frustration, but his grief floated too close to the surface. He sank onto his desk chair as the tears started to fall. He summoned the precious red handkerchief – the one that Mel had transformed from black to its current colour – to catch the droplets before they could hit the desk. Demons didn't cry – definitely not the Lord of Hell. God, what would the others think of him if they saw?

But the Lord of Hell had never lost his beloved angel before. He'd never had one to lose until now and he'd barely had her for a moment before they took her away.

To Hell with everyone and everything. Luce sealed his office to everyone else and lost himself in grief.

# Twenty-Six

Mel rounded a corner to find her wings caught on the rough rocks enclosing a narrow passage. Folding them out of sight, she surveyed the line of shadowy, sad souls blocking her progress. Some of them were shaking where they stood, while others shifted their feet constantly, as if looking for firm ground to stand on from which to plead their case.

The scene reminded her a little of those awaiting judgement at Heaven's gates, but there were no angels or demons to be seen. Perhaps the damned didn't qualify for escorts, Mel thought. Or the escort demons didn't care enough about their charges to wait with them. Neither would have surprised her.

The passage looked too tightly packed with people to squeeze through, so she resolved to wait patiently. The line did appear to be moving, and more swiftly than the line of souls awaiting entrance to Heaven.

She touched the shoulder of the man before her. "Excuse me," she began, "can you please tell me what we're waiting for?"

"Accommodation assignments," the man replied over his shoulder. "There's a boss up ahead who says where you get to stay. Someone said I'll probably be down on Level Three."

"Level Three?" Mel enquired politely.

"Yeah, Level Three. That's where drug addicts go. I mean, I wouldn't have killed all those people if it weren't for the drugs, see? Some I was too high to remember and the others should've known better'n to get between me and the money for another hit.

The girls who wouldn't put out for the punters had it coming, too..."

Mel carefully tucked her hands behind her so she wouldn't touch the man again. The hazy impression she'd received from his mind had initially reminded her of a Jimi Hendrix song, but now that she knew why, she didn't want to know any more of it. How many deaths had resulted from this man's habit? How many lives ruined, how many hurt or... She felt tears streak her cheeks.

"Hey, it's all right, sweetheart. If I had any on me right now, I'd give it to you. It'd send you straight to Heaven, instead of Level Two, where they put the little lusty ones. Pretty girl like you, they'll go easy on you."

She met the eyes of the addict in surprise. He was Hellbound, no mistake, but the man still had a heart, somewhere deep beneath the dark haze. "I'm worried for a friend of mine who's in the deepest level here, I think. I need to see and speak to him. I'm not staying."

His eyes widened. "You're not here for judgement? Fuck me, I heard it was only angels who could leave once they were in. You a real angel?"

Mel lowered her eyes and nodded. "He's here by mistake. I won't leave until I've seen him. The others are waiting in Heaven for me to return with him."

The man snorted and it turned into a phlegmy cough that made him spit on the stone floor. "Fuck. First I ever heard of angels judging someone and making a mistake. Wish I had an angel looking after me. Here, I'm in no hurry. How 'bout we switch places and you go first?"

He sashayed to the side of the passage, ushering her past. Mel thanked him and moved forward.

"OI!" the man's voice rang out. "We got an angel here, says there's been a mistake. Let 'er through!"

Bowed heads lifted and turned to stare curiously at Mel. Embarrassed, she kept her head down.

"I SAID MOVE!" he hollered. "Who's in a hurry to get into Hell five minutes faster? Fuck'n MOVE for the angel!"

Shuffling footsteps scraped on stone as

people moved aside. Thankful that she'd already hidden her wings, she sidled past as many as she could, trying not to meet anyone's eyes. She didn't want to see inside any of their souls — just the first man in the queue had saddened her enough. She'd sink under the knowledge of all their sins. So much harm...

"I'm coming for you, Luce," she murmured. "I won't leave you mired in this despair. Hold on, my love." Determination drove her steps, more sure with every word. Luce needed her and if she faltered through fear, he would pay the price — a debt she would need to repay.

With all her will bent on the soul at her destination, Mel didn't see the body before her until she bumped into him.

"I'm sorry," she said, stopping.

"Yeah, everyone's sorry, but not sorry enough, which is why you ended up here," he said roughly. "What did you do that everyone's so eager to see you judged for?"

Mel glanced back and saw the crowded passage, full of people craning to get a good view. Her courage failed. "I'm here for Luce," she whispered.

Something snaked around her waist and tightened, threatening to crush her. "It's Lord Lucifer here, and you'd best remember it. The Lord of Hell doesn't forgive or forget. And neither do I." The tail gave her a squeeze. "Now, tell me the truth. I'll know if you lie. Who are you and what was the worst sin you committed?"

"I ate the last dozen Valentine's chocolates by myself and didn't give them to my colleagues." A searing pain deep in her soul made her want to double over, but the man's tail held her upright. "Luce," she wailed weakly. The pain wasn't hers but his. A sudden stab made her scream, yet her skin was unharmed. What could hurt Luce so badly? "Hold on, Luce," she mumbled as the pain overwhelmed her.

The grip on her body lessened, but the pain didn't change. If anything, it grew stronger. Mel felt stone under her knees and she forced her eyes open. She couldn't fall. She needed to find Luce. A heavily built man glared down at her. "Who are you?" he demanded. "Judgement is worse for those who don't confess completely!"

His name surfaced in her thoughts. "Minos," she managed to say.

"Yeah, that's me," he replied. "Who in Hell are you?"

"I'm Mel." Her voice died to a whisper.

"Nope, don't know a Mel. Try again," the man said.

Her soul ached again. "Luce. I need to find Luce. He's hurting..."

"The Lord of Hell hurts a lot of people, girl – it's his job. Tell me your name or you can go wait at the back of the line until you remember it. I'm in no hurry and there's plenty more where you came from."

Mel swallowed, trying to block the pain. It felt as if, somehow, Luce was doing the same. Welcoming the reprieve, she forced the words out quickly before it returned. "Lady Muriel of the Hashmallim. I'm here to see Lucifer."

Minos doubled over with laughter. "That's a good one, girl. The day I see an angel like her down here...hahahaha...pull the other one!"

Looking deep into his eyes, Mel gritted her teeth and said, "Angels don't lie, Minos."

A fresh wave of pain punched her in the gut and she fell into blackness, haunted by the sound of her own scream.

# Twenty-Seven

Luce had been there – drifting in the dark – but he'd disappeared. So much pain...

The light was dim and the pain was gone. The pallet beneath her rustled as Mel shifted. Straw covered by coarse cloth, with the solidity of stone supporting the lot. No pillows. This wasn't the bed of a modern man.

Feeling a little bruised, she sat up, wincing. Her body was intact – that, at least, she could tell. She squinted at her arms and her chest, remembering the agony that had taken her consciousness. Mel couldn't remember the last time she'd fainted. She reached out for Luce, but she only felt him faintly – as if he was asleep, or heavily shielded from her, though not far away. Somewhere below...

"I ask your forgiveness, Lady Muriel." Silhouetted in the cave entrance, Minos knelt with his head bowed. "I hope I didn't harm you. The stories some of those damned souls come up with...I thought I'd heard them all. And a girl claiming to be you...I'm sorry I didn't recognise you immediately."

Mel clambered to her unsteady feet. "It's been more than three thousand years, Minos. You were human then."

His eyes stayed firmly fixed on the floor as he shook his head. "It's no excuse. You remembered me."

"If you'd told me last week that today I'd be talking to you in Hell, I wouldn't have believed it. Yet here I am and I won't leave until I've seen Luce." She regarded the large man with thoughtful eyes. "Can you help me find him, Minos? It would certainly make my task easier."

Another heavy head-shake. "Lord Lucifer is in his lair, in the deepest part of Hell, where I can't go. Word is that he doesn't want to be disturbed." Minos lowered his voice. "The rumour I've heard is that he suffered some sort of setback on the surface. Something to do with a girl."

Mel smiled and waited.

Minos stared at Mel. "He didn't try to seduce you, did he? I mean, you calling him...that...and coming here to see him might make people think...Michael would be ready to declare war on him again, if he knew!"

Mel's suspicions rose. "What do you know about Michael and Luce? And where did you hear it?"

She watched in fascination as Minos clasped his hands as if in prayer – though his people never prayed in this way. "Please, don't be angry with me. I have a beer or two with Peter every other week – he's fond of barley beer and I know where to get the best, just like we used to have at home – and occasionally Michael comes, too. Judgement is a thankless job and sometimes you just need to talk to someone who understands, or you'd go mad." He paused, as if waiting for Mel to say something, but she simply smiled. "Okay. From what Michael's said when he's had a horn too many, he's terrified that his premonitions will come true."

Mel was confused by the reference to horns, so it took her a moment to realise that drinking vessels were the least of her worries. "What premonitions? Michael's been getting premonitions about me? Since when?"

"Always the same one. Since just before the Fall," Minos whispered. He glanced around, as if looking for eavesdroppers. When he seemed satisfied, he stood and crept into the room. He gestured at the pallet. "May I?"

Mel nodded.

He sank into the straw, shifting his crown so he could scratch his thinning hair beneath it.

Mel seated herself beside him, curling her knees to her chest as she rested her back against the limestone wall.

"You know in the Heavenly War, that Michael and Lucifer each led an army?" he began, before looking sheepish. "Of course you know. I've just seen so many new demons that weren't around then. Michael met with you and he agreed with your idea of offering Hell to Lucifer so he'd surrender without a fight, what with the offer of his own realm to run and all. Well, on the eve before battle, Michael dreamed of you. He saw you meet with Lucifer and Lucifer fell to his knees before you. The dream ended with you walking into Hell. And when Michael donned his armour the next morning, he swore he'd keep you from Lucifer, so he could never lead you into Hell." He swallowed. "Your brother's army won and he banished Lucifer here, never to enter Heaven again, but he couldn't keep him from Earth. Every time he heard rumours that Lucifer had returned to Earth to make another bid for power, he sent someone to investigate..."

Raphael, Mel thought. Michael was in a lot more trouble than she'd realised. "Why haven't you told Luce this? He's the Lord of Hell and your boss."

Minos reddened and stared at his lap. "Lord

Lucifer never asks for my advice on matters of strategy or policy. All he wants from me are numbers – who went where and how many – and I send them to one of his senior demons every month. I believe he finds my knowledge of politics...outdated. He doesn't know I had the best advisor any king could ever have, in the past, present or future, and I learned more from her in one human lifetime than he has in all his time to date!" He'd risen to his feet and Mel saw the king she'd known so many centuries ago. "Leave while you can, Lady Muriel. I'll tell him nothing. Michael will be relieved to see you home safe and the world will be in the right hands again."

"Not all leaders see mine as the right hands, Minos. Your own grandson..." Mel broke off.

"You mean my namesake – the murderer of Athenian children? I think he's down on Level Eight and I hope he rots there," Minos spat. He turned worried eyes to Mel. "You mean he did worse things than that?"

"He betrayed me," she admitted. "He listened to my counsel on countless occasions and sometimes even asked me to administer justice to his people. There was a woman...ah, she was accused of some terrible crimes that she didn't commit. It was so long ago – I don't even remember her name. She was the last in a long line of people he asked me to judge that day. I pronounced judgement in front of a large crowd that had gathered in the court at Knossos – I told them that she was innocent. I wasn't aware that the king had promised them her death in order to save the guilty party – a woman he'd taken a fancy to. I stated one judgement, their king another...and when he heard, he screamed at the already angry crowd that I must have helped the woman. The crowd...it was a riot. I tried to shield her with my own body, for I knew that the body I wore didn't matter and I could construct another. I couldn't protect her. They tore our bodies apart. And I've never been able to speak in public since, for I remember the feeling of all those eyes on me, then all those hands tearing, tugging, gouging...and the sound of her screaming as they did the same to her." Mel shuddered delicately. "Even that small crowd today was enough to freeze my voice in my throat as it dropped me to my knees. Lady Muriel, advisor to chieftains, secretary-generals, emperors, presidents and kings, but unable to voice a single word when a dozen might hear me." She gave a snort of laughter.

"I'll see him moved to Level Nine with the other hypocrites and traitors," Minos swore, clenching his fists. "You should leave, Lady Muriel, before Lord Lucifer hears you're here and tries to keep you. The world needs you whispering in their leaders' ears – as I know, all too well."

"I can't leave, Minos. I must see Luce and I won't stop until I have. Michael's premonition – it has come to pass, for I have entered Hell, as you see. I won't leave until my task is complete." She patted his shoulder. She sensed only concern – not the despair so prevalent among the others in Hell, or the darkness surrounding the demons' souls. Minos was neither damned nor demon – but not quite an angel, either.

"What do I tell Peter and Michael? Michael's going to be furious." Minos wrung his hands.

"Tell them...tell Michael that we will have

words when I return. Sending an innocent man to Hell in order to save his sister from a fate he had no right to prevent...tell him I will speak to him again only when I have healed the damage he has done, as I see fit. He will wait for my summons." Mel heard her voice resonate in the little cave, as if she were pronouncing judgement on her brother. In a way, perhaps she was.

Minos licked his lips nervously. "Are you sure? He's got that sword and it can do a fair bit of damage when he's angry. I can handle him, but a lady like yourself..."

Mel rose to her feet. Her voice was soft as she said, "Are you a gambling man, Minos? Michael tells you I will not leave Hell, based on an incomplete premonition, and I tell you I will – with its Lord, no less. Not a premonition – a promise. On whom would you bet your harvest?"

Minos grinned, his eyes lighting up with her reflected radiance. "Lady Muriel, I'd bet my kingdom on you. I bet Michael spits his beer out when I tell him so, too. I wish you well." He bowed deeply. "If you are ever in need of my assistance, only call and I will be there. If you change your mind and wish to leave Hell, summon me and I will escort you home." He winked. "Lord Lucifer owes me a favour or two, and I'd happily collect on them to repay my debt to you."

Mel's laughter sounded loud in the small space. "You did learn a lot, didn't you? Thank you, Minos. If you could point the way to Luce's lair, that would be plenty for the moment."

She followed Minos through a labyrinth of narrow caverns and passages until he stopped. "This is Level Two, Lady Muriel. Once again, I wish you well – and I hope to see you soon in Heaven, for a horn of good barley beer." The man bowed and disappeared into the dark.

Mel took a deep breath and set off once more, wishing she knew what had caused Luce such unbearable pain – and why his soul seemed so silent now.

# Twenty-Eight

Damned and down here, where no angel would ever find him, to taunt him about the joy he'd almost had. Mel would never follow him here – wouldn't or couldn't. He didn't want her here, either – this was no place for an angel like her. Her realm was Heaven; his was Hell. Surely she'd seen that in the last moments before her body sublimated.

Angels and demons didn't get to live happily ever after. Destiny wouldn't allow it – and Destiny was a bitch to him on a good day. Mel deserved better – better than he could ever be. She'd soon see that, if her soul had been able to escape to Heaven. The other angels would help her. Heaven was full of those who hated him. It wouldn't be long before she did, too – unless she was dead.

Dead or indifferent – did it matter which? With his Hellish weapon, he'd driven away all hope of a future with her. He'd never wanted to drag her down here to be with him – nothing could be allowed to taint someone as pure as Mel. Luce fingered the prongs on his bident. A thin patina of Mel's blood still stained the weapon, though it had dried and wasn't likely to drip on the desk.

Idly, he wondered when this desk had last been cleaned – his desk in the office on Earth was sprayed and wiped daily, after Mel had turned him down and pointed out its poor hygiene. She'd even made him laugh, though he'd been furious at the time. Mel had made each day worth living, not just something to be endured until his next goal was achieved. What were his goals, anyway? Just a way of keeping score until the world ended.

But that world with Mel had been one he never wanted to see end.

The work Christmas parties, in the hotel and with the carnivorous swans. He'd planned on avoiding or sleeping through them both, as he did every year. Yet he'd seen her heading off, her arms full of alcohol, and his heart had leaped at the thought of a party – any party – with her, alcohol-uninhibited and...aaah... She'd laughed and enjoyed herself, inspiring him to do the same. With her help, he'd stroked a swan – one that would have devoured his fingers.

It was Mel. Always, it was Mel. What creature wouldn't lie down and let her have her way with him? Heavenly, for she'd never hurt him. Hell, he'd even reacted like the swans when she'd stroked his dark wings – what he'd give for her to do it again. Any part of him. Or a kiss...

She wouldn't. Mel would never touch him again. He was too far beneath her. In the dark. Damned. For letting her die. He deserved it. All this and more.

He touched the blood on the bident again.

Her blood.

Could the Lord of Hell's weapon kill an angel, like Michael's flaming sword could force one to fall against his will? He could think of no better test subject than himself – for no angel deserved to die as much as he did. If the bident could kill an angel, then his surely had stolen her life. Maybe Mel would be waiting for him...

Oh God, what would he give for it to be true? Everything. Even his life. For her.

He pulled up his sleeves, then took his shirt off altogether. He wouldn't need it any more. He wanted to plunge the damn thing through his heart, if he still had one, skewering it like some sort of spiritual satay stick with his heart beside hers.

Practicality won out – he wasn't sure he had the strength to push the long-handled weapon through his own breast.

Was it darker in the room, or was it just his eyes dimming?

The bloodied bident prongs, like obscene nipples piercing her shirt through her breasts. Oh God.

He should have known they'd never let him have her.

"Hold on, my love," she'd said, believing everything would be all right. He could almost hear her voice saying it now.

He buried his face in his hands. Nothing could stop the tears. Look how the Lord of Hell cried for the loss of one woman. One, after more than a hundred and fifty thousand – his downfall had been the woman who'd made him rise. A woman so kind she'd seemed incredibly innocent, instead of so worldly-wise that even he couldn't fault her. He'd held out hope of love and life with her in Heaven, for she'd said it was possible. For the first time, she'd been wrong.

Luce reached for her shirt and breathed deep, savouring her perfume. Heaven smelled of her. Myrrh... He hoped the weapon was capable of killing him, for he didn't want to wake without her.

"Luce," she'd called him, her voice caressing the name he used among humans on the surface. In his heart, she was calling him again. He couldn't refuse her.

He dragged the fork from the desk, holding it between his thighs so it came to his chest. No, he couldn't impale himself as he had her. With a dagger or a sword, perhaps. This had to be the instrument of his death, as it had been hers. If only he could work out how.

Lifting his arms above his head, he prayed for guidance – for what he feared would never come. Oh God...he was crying again.

He dropped his hands and felt the sting of a sharp point pierce his palm. He watched the blood well up, a red rivulet that trickled down his wrist. His prayer was answered. It would be slower this way, but Heaven knew he deserved the pain.

Luce lined his arms up, so each barb centred on the vein bisecting his wrists. He lifted his arms once more, clenching his hands together as he concentrated on keeping them steady. Please, let him strike true on the first time. The tears were flowing too fast for him to see clearly any more.

Mel. Oh God, Mel...

Luce drove his arms down, grunting as bronze met bone. Blood spurted, but the pain was nothing compared to the hole where his heart had been. Empty without her.

The blood would flow faster if he pulled his wrists off the barbs. He'd see her sooner.

Gritting his teeth so hard he thought they'd crack, Luce wrenched his arms up. He saw chunks of his own flesh impaled on the weapon that had been his, before he toppled over onto the floor and forgot all about it.

Nothing hurt like the loneliness inside. He crawled away to feel the cold stone beneath his body one last time, bringing his arms before his face so he could watch his lifeblood draining out through the gaping holes; marking the flow of time until he could hold her in his arms again, or oblivion would claim him and he'd never know this pain again.

Please, let this old demon die. He has nothing left to live for.

"Luce," she called again, fainter this time.

"I'm coming, sweet Melody," he said, before he sank deep into a darkness from which he hoped never to wake up.

# Twenty-Nine

Mel didn't want to enter the next cavern. It looked like it was full of people lying on the floor, having fits. They were spread out on the stone floor, much like the others had been in the cave pool, but these ones were moving jerkily as if they had no control over their own bodies.

She knelt to touch the shoulder of the nearest body – a young woman, she guessed. Immediately, the cavern roof vanished in thick cloud and a spattering of hail headed for her face. She felt the force of the wind on her body, blowing them both away from the skinny young man the girl reached for. The girl's wail of despair as she was torn away from the boy before she could even touch him rasped on Mel's heart. Mel let go of the girl and both the storm and the boy vanished.

Her hands trembling, Mel reached for an older woman crouching on all fours and crying. The storm resumed – just as fiercely as before – only this time the woman was being swept away from what appeared to be her whole family, as a man banged her relentlessly from behind. Mel released this woman, too, and the rutting man vanished along with the children shrieking for their mother.

Mel's heart ached for all of them. They knew despair she never could. Even if Luce was just a faint presence somewhere deep and distant, she wasn't being forced away from him. Quite the contrary – she knew she was getting closer. What could they possibly have done to deserve such despair for eternity? She could feel the grief etched into these souls. Why couldn't this be enough?

She stumbled through the bucking bodies, not wanting to touch another. Yet a familiar face caught her eye – a ruler who had ignored her advice in order to pursue his lust, much like Minos' grandson and namesake. Without thinking, she reached for his shoulder.

The storm seemed to centre on this man, who saw others outside the whirlwind and reached for them as they appeared and vanished. What also seemed to vanish were bits of the man's body – swept up in the twister encircling him and whirled away until they, too, vanished from sight as he screamed. Mel watched the man's hand slowly disintegrate, a piece at a time, before it was followed by his genitals. Repulsed, she yanked her hand back.

In life, the man had ordered all lepers to be executed, for his own infirmity had been his greatest fear. Now, by some irony, he was forced to feel his own body fall apart as those he'd loved or lusted after in life looked on without helping him.

But that had been centuries ago. Centuries. No...at least a millennium. Maybe close to two.

How long was enough? Eternity was too much.

"LUCE!" Mel shouted. "Why don't you stop this? Suffering must have an end some time!"

As always, there was no answer. Incensed, she reached for him. Faint, but there; despair and then...gone.

"No!" she gasped, falling to her knees. "Don't you disappear. Luce!"

Illusions, Mel told herself. All the despair was an illusion and somehow she'd let it wash over her. She knew where Hell's illusions originated and they would answer to her. "Spklt! Lift the illusions in this cavern," she shouted with her voice and then deeper, with her spirit.

"Lady, Spklt has Lord's orders..." The imp appeared amid the bodies, accompanied by many more, as his words touched her soul.

"MY order is to lift the illusion. It is too strong and I say it is enough."

"Agreement with Lord..." The imp's thoughts drifted off.

"Tell him I ordered it and let him pursue me," Mel insisted, hoping this more open challenge to his authority might bring him out of hiding. A whole level of Hell disrupted.

"As you will, Lady. Lord will be angry. Very amusing." The imp bowed, as did his colleagues. They straightened and stilled, and Mel caught a glimpse of the imps' shared excitement at seeing Luce aroused in anger and lust. They hoped for an epic battle, but they would settle for explosive sex.

Mel couldn't help laughing. Nothing stirred up trouble as much as an imp – and their mischievous imaginations would put a human author to shame. She'd never heard of most of the things they hoped she and Luce would do.

Luce. She reached for him again, but still she couldn't find him. She refused to give up. "I'm coming to save you from yourself, for I won't lose you, my love," she murmured. "And if you take love advice from any of the imps today, you'll have to find yourself a human contortionist, because I will not..." She heard the imps' amusement and shut the thought down.

She glanced at the prone and supine souls, seeing some start to move toward their peers, murmuring names. Mel heard a wet kiss and whispered endearments, along with some pet names she'd have preferred not to know.

Wondering what a pookie was, and why it seemed so essential to so many of these damned souls, she stepped through them to the tunnel that led to the lower levels.

Let Luce see her handiwork. If he wanted to maintain control over Hell, then he'd have to come to her. If he made her walk all the way to his lair...she'd ensure all Hell broke loose above him.

Mel felt the imps' agreement. They would be her allies in this, for there was no amusement for them while Luce locked himself in his lair.

Behind her, she heard a moan of pleasure and not pain. She quickened her steps.

# Thirty

A bark broke the silence, followed by what sounded like a pack of dogs. Mel headed in the direction the sound had come from – she had heard tales of Cerberus, but the dog never left his guard post. She knew her path lay beyond the creature, so she summoned her courage and sought him out.

The once-pitiful, poorly mutated puppy did indeed have three heads and all were barking, creating a cacophony of echoes in the cave. The huge creature wasn't chained or restrained in any way, but only its heads moved toward Mel, alternately sniffing and baying like three separate dogs. She saw the food bowls at its feet, but they were all empty. The poor creature was hungry.

Concentrating, she summoned a snack for the beast – some pork sausages she'd planned to cook with Luce on the weekend. Perhaps the meat would see better use here. She held them out. Two heads extended toward her, while the third hung back, afraid. The two stretched, sniffed...then snarled and fell on one another, fighting over the meat neither of them could reach. All the while, the beast's four feet didn't move. Three heads controlling one body – poor, confused creature, Mel thought. She split the sausages into three portions, tossing them into the dishes. No wonder it was so huge, with three heads to eat but only one body to sustain. It didn't look like anyone had fed him recently, though, as she watched him devour the fresh meat.

All around them, water plinked and flowed to the floor, muffling the sounds of mastication.

One of the beast's heads abandoned his meal to deliver a menacing growl at her.

"That's not a good idea," she said, fixing her eyes on the growling head. With all her attention on Cerberus, Mel jumped when she felt something damp clamp around her ankle. The firm grip anchored her to the ground as she tried to twist around to see what had seized her. Something even slimier enveloped her toes.

It was a mud-covered man, his mouth sucking blissfully at her foot. Horrified, Mel pulled out of his grasp and shifted closer to Cerberus. Two heads were now growling at the man, straining to snap at him.

The man subsided into the mud from whence he'd come, a foetid swamp that stretched as far as Mel could see in the dim cavern. Wondering where the clay had come from to create a swamp so deep in a cave, Mel saw a human figure rise from the muck and relieve itself, before sinking down into the filth once more. The surface writhed with bodies, Mel realised, horrified. She wondered what sort of sins those on this level had committed.

Did toe-sucking count? She couldn't quite recall if that was a sin or not. Surely it wasn't worse than the lust that had condemned those on Level Two. Mel didn't want to touch one of the damned to find out – their crimes might be far worse than she'd thought. Perhaps there were some things she didn't need to know.

Mel looked at the expanse of mud, thinking she'd found the sludge layer of the world's largest septic tank. After curry night in the demons' barracks, she decided, remembering the septic flight school explosion she'd heard about when she worked in the HELL Corporation office. No wonder the demons had found the incident funny – when they were accustomed to this sort of sewage every day.

She wondered if there was a way around, not wanting to soil herself with any more of the nightsoil than necessary. The suspicious mud on her foot and ankle smelled awful already. Only one way to find out...

Mel shook out her wings and rose to hover over the mire. No, it looked like Level Three was wall-to-wall mud. Sighing, she figured her wings could do with the exercise. After all, she rarely had an excuse to fly on Earth. Dodging the stalactites would be a fun test of her rusty flight skills.

Stranded beside the cesspool, Cerberus started barking again, the sound echoing through the cavern as she left him behind.

"Come out and feed your dog, Luce — and get someone to see to your septic tank. If anything needs pumping out, it's that," Mel said softly, wishing he'd hear her and dreading that he wouldn't, even if she shouted.

# Thirty-One

Mel heard the sounds of shouting from up ahead and landed lightly on her feet, folding her wings out of sight so that she might better navigate the narrow passage between one level and the next. She emerged from the tunnel into a cavern filled with yelling people. Thousands of them, all seemingly engaged in heated arguments and shoving matches with each other over...nothing. Mel touched the woman nearest her and was transported into an ancient, bustling marketplace. The woman seemed to alternate between shouting at the merchant for the items she ardently desired and those crowding around her for getting in her way. Mel released the woman as a man bumped into her and began shouting at her. Mel glimpsed a modern department store, emblazoned with signs that read, 'Black Friday SALE,' before the man took umbrage at a woman who appeared to be lifting a foot spa from a display table, leaving Mel alone to vent his spleen on her instead.

Mad. They're all mad, Mel decided, trying to squeeze through the milling crowd.

A tinkling sound grew louder as she crossed the cavern, the only high note among the deeper voices of the crowd. Like small bells, Mel thought, wondering why they were present. Their purpose could hardly be anything good.

Wishing she was tall enough to see over more of the crowd, Mel moved through them as best she could, following the chiming toward its source. She tripped over a box and nearly fell, but regained her balance in time. Reaching down, Mel lifted the foot spa box she'd seen earlier, wondering what such a strange item was doing here. Figuring she'd best get it out of harm's way, she carried it with her through the crowd.

The throng thinned as she approached the far wall and Mel saw that the cavern had a raised dais, with rough steps cut up one side. She ascended, knowing she was close. Laying the box by the wall, she approached what looked like a waist-high frame with objects suspended from it with string. Closer, she saw what made the sound. Each object was a chiming cat toy being vigorously pawed and batted by a belled calico cat. Their poses reminded her of the waving good luck cats she'd seen in Japan – Maneki Neko, the statues were called. But these were the real thing – live cats, willingly waving for infinitely greater luck than any statue could provide.

Why cats? she wondered, unable to resist a closer look and a chance to play with them. The moment she dropped to her knees, the nearest cat left its toy to saunter over for some investigation. The beast sniffed and then licked Mel's soiled ankle until no mud remained – just the faint fishy scent of the cat's saliva.

Laughing, Mel summoned some fish to repay her cleaning companion – some of her lunch pouches of tuna, tipping the contents onto the stone ledge. All chiming ceased as the other cats scented the treat and padded to join the impromptu feast.

Wishing she could spend more time with the cats, but knowing she'd have to continue, Mel thought of the box of ping pong balls in her shed. Perhaps they'd like to play with those, too – especially with such a large space. Bringing the box to her hands, she waited for the cats to finish cleaning themselves before she upended the box. Balls spun erratically in all directions, ably assisted by enthused cats.

Mere seconds passed before both cats and balls had vanished from the dais and they were careening between the crazed shoppers on the floor below. Mel watched, enchanted.

"My luck!" shrieked a voice. It belonged to a dark-haired, diminutive man clutching a wad of what looked like betting slips. "Where is my luck? My kitties. My kitties!" The man's hands fluttered like frightened birds, showering the stone with paper.

"It's all right. They're still here. I'm sure they'll return when they get hungry," Mel said.

"But the battle! The epic battle! Bets have just closed and the next ten minutes will decide the winner. And they're not even interested!" the little man insisted shrilly.

A half-dozen cats couldn't distract thousands of people, surely, Mel thought, scanning the crowd. The quiet, still crowd. By all that was holy...how could a playing cat capture the fascination of so many? Even Mel thought it a miracle of sorts. Who'd have thought?

"They're not fighting for the foot spa! The bets are on who wins the foot spa today!" he wailed.

Mel glanced at the box that he hadn't seemed to have noticed. "That would be me. It was just sitting on the ground, so I lifted it out of harm's way. I must admit I've never used one before and my feet are a little sore from walking bare on the stone today. Are they hard to use?"

"You? Who are you?" the man spat.

Something about the way he moved and pouted reminded Mel of Persi. "You're my cousin Demeter's other son, Ploutos," she said slowly. "I'm Mel."

"Mel? Mel?" Ploutos squawked. "I don't know any Mel – OH!" Dark eyes grew round. "Lady Muriel! What the Hell are you doing here?"

Mel managed a smile. "Looking for Lucifer. I need to speak to him."

"What will Lord Lucifer say when he sees this?" Ploutos wailed, waving at the happy, cat-watching denizens of Level Four.

"Tell him an interfering angel came in and disrupted your perfectly run part of Hell," Mel replied. "The sooner I find him, the less disruption I'll cause to his realm."

Ploutos swallowed noisily. "Yes, Lady Muriel. I must warn you, though. Don't use the foot spa. Just leave it here. It's faulty. This is Hell, after all. The nearest relaxing foot massage is probably in a day spa thousands of kilometres away. I hope you get it, Lady Muriel. Lord Lucifer is...surlier than usual, lately. He sees no one and none have entered his lair in some time. I wish you every success, but an angry Lord Lucifer is not something you should see. My half-sister, Persi, seems to have some sort of crazy crush on him, but even she's scared of his temper. Yet she keeps coming here, wanting to see him..."

Mel raised her eyebrows. "Persi? Here? That's...disturbing news. She should be running the HELL Corporation back on Earth, where I left her."

"She has it bad for Lord Lucifer and she's determined to have him at any cost. Can you speak to her? Tell her what she's risking?"

"When I see her next, I will certainly speak to her. The last place she should be is here in Hell. Not if she wants to be an angel..." Mel said.

"This is why we need you so much. Who would do what you do if Lord Lucifer...if he...I'm sorry, Lady Muriel, but his fury is frightening. If he summoned all the powers of Hell and unleashed them on you...he could do untold damage. I wouldn't want him to hurt you."

Mel laughed. "Thank you, Ploutos, but I

think I've seen his temper already. Honestly, Luce is about as dangerous as those cats."

Ploutos managed a sickly smile. "I hope you're right, Lady Muriel. I wouldn't want to be in your place."

Mel nodded and decided she'd dallied long enough. She was barely halfway through Hell and the ominous silence from Luce was worrying her. Bidding farewell to Ploutos, she set off for the lower levels of Hell, where she knew Luce had to be hiding.

# Thirty-Two

The mercantile battle behind her may have ceased, but Mel heard more fighting ahead. She wondered if they were fighting over another faulty foot spa or whether there was a far greater prize at stake. Under the clash of metal and shouting voices, she could hear the bass gurgle of water. Standing at the edge of the cavern, her first impression was of the aftermath of the Battle of Arausio. Thousands of men struggling in a river while they sank beneath the weight of their armour, fighting each other all the way down. The Rhone hadn't been so swampy – this underground river looked more like the Styx, though Thessaly was a world away from where she was now.

Mel sniffed carefully, but this didn't smell the same as Level Three's sewage. Not fresh, certainly, but more like artesian water than wastewater. The taint of blood in the air did turn her stomach a little, though.

"Are you looking to place your bet, too?" a voice said. "You're cutting it close. Battle ends in an hour."

"What happens when the battle ends?" Mel asked.

"Same thing that happens at the end of every day. Everyone stops fighting, we count up all the missing bits and announce who lost the least limbs and drowned the fewest times. Wait a few hours, until everything's grown back in the morning, then start over. Are you new?" The tunic-clad demon squinted at her.

Mel smiled. "I wouldn't say that, though I don't believe we've met before."

"Phlegyas. I used to be a king, once, and now I'm just king of the moat. All that rutting fool Apollo's fault. The man thought the sun shone out of his arse, but my daughter knew otherwise. She picked someone better and the idiot got jealous. So now I pole a boat in the dark, in between taking bets on the battle below." He shrugged. "Such is life."

"Phlegyas...Thessaly? I think I was working with Minos then...your reign was cut short before I got a chance to meet you," Mel said.

"Ah, I remember those days. Seems like only yesterday..." Phlegyas shook his head. "Now they all want minions, weapons of mass destruction and mobile phones. HA! They get a spear, a sword and whatever armour they can find that fits. If they want padding to stop the armour from chafing, they have to source that themselves, or they can go naked." He appraised Mel from top to toe. "I'm not sure we have armour contoured for your shape, but it looks like you're already dressed for the more berserker style of battle. Good luck to you, lady. Probably the safest battle you'll ever be in – no rape and pillaging here. Just hacking off limbs and such. Wait until this one's over and see if you can find yourself a sword small enough. You'll get the hang of things eventually." When he turned to point at the small pile of weapons remaining, Mel saw that his tunic was hiked up at the back over his tail, baring his backside. Sun didn't shine out of his behind, either.

"Oh, I'm not here to fight, Phlegyas. Nor do I wish to place a wager on the outcome of today's battle. I'm seeking Lucifer. I must see him before I leave."

"You sure? I can give you good odds. The favourite is...that big bastard there." Phlegyas pointed at a hulking man who was fighting off three muddy figures in waist-deep mud not far from them. He whirled, sending a wave of muddy water that reached the shore and splattered at Mel's feet, leaving splotches of mud up her thigh.

Mel glanced down and sighed. Between the sewage, mud and cat saliva, she really wanted a bath some time soon. The sooner she found Luce, the sooner she could go home. Maybe he'd agree to share her shower. That was something they hadn't done yet.

"No, I need to get going. I don't have time

to watch this battle." Mel nodded at a boat, pulled up on shore. "Will you take me across the river to where the next level is?"

"Not until the battle's over!" Phlegyas said, staring at her. "They'll drag the boat under and add us to the casualty list. I'll take you when it's done, but not before. You could always row over yourself...I won't go near the water until they call a ceasefire."

Mel shrugged. "I guess I'll fly, same as I did on Level Three. Tell me which way to go, please."

Phlegyas' eyes seemed to widen further. "Fly? You some sort of fallen angel or something? You should already know all the lower levels are through Dis, over that side." He pointed into the dark.

Mel laughed, shaking her wings out and letting them lift her higher. "Thank you. No, I haven't fallen yet and I won't if I can help it. That way? So be it."

The cavern ceiling was low, so her wingtips brushed the stone even as her toes skimmed the water. Muddy water splashed over her skin as combatants burst from the water, first fighting one another and then reaching for her. A long wolf-whistle cut through the other sounds, originating from a man with a swastika tattoo on his shoulder. Heads surfaced from the water and more whistles sounded like eerie echoes, pursuing her across the water.

The sounds of battles ceased. "Angel," came the gasped cry from hundreds of throats. "The angel of victory."

"Angel of mud, more like!" Mel called back over her shoulder. The shore approached and it was only a narrow strip of sand, ending in a seemingly solid cavern wall. It didn't look like there was access to the lower levels from here. Mel landed and strode closer to investigate.

# Thirty-Three

"What in Hell? More gates? What does Hell need more gates for? Everyone's stuck in the horrible delusions in their own heads." Mel glared at the barrier, stretching up to meet the cavern roof above her head.

"It's your turn to deal."

"No, yours. I did the last round. You need to learn to shuffle better, Kas."

"I shuffle just fine! You're the one who can't shuffle, Mo – you dealt me that last straight."

The clink hiss of beer bottles being opened,

before the clink of glass.

"To Lady Luck!"

"To her deciding Kas is a poxy whore and smiling at us again!"

"OI!"

Mel laughed softly as she headed toward the voices, her feet almost silent on the cold stone. She saw them before they saw her – three fallen angels, sitting at a square table, drinking beer and talking so loudly they never heard her approach.

"Can one of you open the gate, please?" she called.

"Holy Hell, is that an angel?"

"Fuck, she's naked. No angel would be crazy enough to walk through here without clothes. She'd have Lord Lucifer on her in no time."

"How come he gets all the best girls?"

"He is the Lord of Hell. Must be the title."

"Nah, guys, that's Mel. She'd freeze his balls before she'd sleep with him. Mel! Come have some beer with us," one of the men invited.

"Who's Mel?" she heard a doubtful voice say.

"She's the one who saved me from the crazy harpy in HR. The one who stabbed me with her shoe over some paper. She's no ordinary angel. The rest look through us demons like we aren't really there – but she's different. She acts like she's one of us, only nicer."

"No angel would do that. We're scum to them – as if we'd make them fall if we so much as soiled their eyeballs with a single glance."

Mel heard Merihim's unmistakeable laugh. "You haven't met Mel, then. She went into an adult shop with Lili to get Gerry's mankini for his birthday. They were having a sale on all the Fetish Fantasy range for some bondage book release – everything out on display, including some toys I'd never heard of. Lili said she barely blushed."

A vision of latex tentacles crept into Mel's mind and she banished it quickly. She hadn't needed to know what they were for then and she definitely didn't need to know now. "What sort of beer are you drinking?" she asked, moving closer.

"Duvel, of course! We have plenty. You look like you need a drink," Asmodeus said, flicking the cap off with his claws. He held the bottle out to her.

Mel admitted she was thirsty and took a deep draught. The beer certainly satisfied her thirst – she'd left the stream far behind, many circles before. She'd lost count somewhere along the way, too – but it didn't matter. Luce was on the other side of that gate – that she knew for certain.

"What was the book? Was it that one with the numbers? Fifty lashes or something?" Kasyade asked.

Merihim shook his head. "Nah, a new release. Something about monsters."

"Monsters in the dark?" Mel suggested, taking another sip. "Sex slavery and sadism?"

"That's the one!" Merihim exclaimed. "It sounded really dark, hence the toy sale."

Mel tried not to laugh. "I heard the hero's name was Quincy. It can't be that dark."

All three men stared at her as she took another drink. "You've read it?" Asmodeus asked, looking shocked.

Mel did laugh this time. "No, not my style. Ana from HR had a copy and she and Lili were discussing it. They both really liked it." She shrugged. "I mean, you guys deal with corporal punishment every day here. It must get boring."

"No, we're not on punishment detail," Asmodeus said quietly. "We do guard duty, mostly – here on the inner gate, or relieving some of the inner-circle demons when they're up on the surface. Ana and Lili are into some of the more physical roles here – I guess they like it." He drank so deeply he finished his beer.

He threw the empty across the cave, where the bottle shattered on a stalactite. He reached into the cooler box beside the table, looking at Mel. "You finished that fast. Need another one?" He offered a fresh beer.

Mel licked the foam from her lips. "Thank you. You're right, I did need that. Can you tell me how I open the gate?"

"What for?" Kasyade scoffed. "Nothing in there but the damned and the Lord of Hell himself, and he's in the nastiest mood I've seen yet. Chewed me out for not feeding his bloody dog while he was off with that little princess he left in charge!" He snorted. "Bullshit, too. The dog wasn't hungry – he'd just finished dinner when I got there, with all sorts of stinking offal. Wouldn't eat it at all."

Mel tried to cover the huge belch threatening to escape. She burped as delicately as she could before admitting, "I fed him. Cerberus looked so sad, I felt sorry for him. I gave him some sausages I'd planned to cook on the weekend. I can always get more once I'm done here."

Asmodeus took a gulp of his beer. "What in Hell are you here for, Mel? I thought you finished up with HELL Corp weeks ago. I figured you'd be back in Heaven with the other angels."

"I'm here to see Luce," she replied cautiously. These were his minions, after all, and not necessarily to be trusted. Luce was the only redeemed demon in Hell.

"What do you want to see that grumpy prick for? Come play cards with us. We'll lend you the money," Merihim offered.

Asmodeus smacked him. "We still owe you for the coffee machine at work. That coffee is heavenly, compared to the instant shit we used to have. We'll pay you back and you can use that money for betting. Can't play poker without some stakes."

"Angels don't gamble," Kasyade sneered. "Not unless they want to fall and stay here permanently. I wouldn't say no to her, but she might have some pasty hypocrite of a cherub waiting for her at home."

"Of course Mel gambles. She won us the office coffee machine on Melbourne Cup Day. C'mon, Mel. One game and we'll show you how to open the gate. Or give you a lift back up to the surface, if you decide after some beer and a hand of poker that Lord Prick isn't worth wasting your time on."

"Okay, it's a deal – a game for the gate, and you can divide my winnings as interest on the loan, if there are any, for I don't need them and I don't have anywhere to carry cash at the moment. I must see Luce – and I won't go home until I've spoken to him. You don't like him much, do you?"

Asmodeus shrugged. "He's the boss. He gets all the girls and gives us all the shit jobs, like feeding the dog, writing government policy in the office and guarding the gate. We do what he says or he gives us to the Corporal girls – and Lili's real mean to demons."

"Lili's here?" Mel asked in surprise.

Kasyade snorted. "Down on Level Seven. Since the little princess took over the office, she's back full-time with us and she's gotten creative. Hell, the only one angrier than her is Lord Prick himself. You'll see – if Lili lets you past. I bet she'd like to get her claws into a sweet little angel like you..."

Merihim snorted with laughter. "Kas, Mel worked for Lili in the office. They get along just fine. Lili's the last of us Mel needs to worry about." He nodded at Mel. "You look dead on your feet. Grab a seat." Merihim pulled out the fourth chair for her and Mel graciously sat, lifting her wings over the back so they sat comfortably. She shook her hair down over her breasts so she wouldn't distract the demons too much with them. She fully intended to play fair.

"Here," Merihim said, pulling a t-shirt out of a bag Mel hadn't seen until now. "It's my change of clothes for the gym in the morning. It's clean – I haven't worn it yet."

Mel smiled and took it. "Thank you. I'll only borrow it – you'll have it back before you need it for the gym."

"Do you know how to play poker?" Kasyade asked. "Five-card draw, fifty-dollar buy-in and two rounds of betting. No limit to the number of raises."

"It's been a long time," Mel admitted. "Would it be okay if I watched a hand or two, just to refresh my memory?"

"Absolutely," Merihim said warmly. He glanced at her empty beer. "Let me get you another drink while you're watching." He opened and passed her another, taking the empty from her fingers.

"Thank you," Mel said, leaning back into her chair. She hadn't realised quite how tired she was until now. It was one Hell of a relief just to sit and do nothing, no more walking, for a few minutes. The beer seemed like a tiny sip of Heaven, too. Good Belgian beer was a luxury she didn't often spend money on.

She watched Kasyade deal, then Merihim

raised and Asmodeus matched him. Kasyade hesitated for a bit before raising, too. The betting ran round the table one more time before the demons traded unwanted cards for new ones and grimaced at the result. Mel found her eyes kept being drawn back to Kasyade, who sat with his arms crossed. She could've sworn he was holding six cards, but she blinked and looked again. No – it was only five, like he was supposed to have.

Merihim folded, but Asmodeus stayed in until the end, when Kasyade's two pair trounced his couple of tens. "Aw, you have all the good luck tonight, Kas," Asmodeus complained. "I swear you've won half my money already and if you keep going like this, I'll be out before the beer's gone!"

"Luck will change with Mel. She's an angel – luck always favours her," Merihim said, smiling at her. "Are you in the next round, Mel?"

"I'd like to watch one more, please," she said. "Then I'll give it a try."

She kept her eyes on Kasyade again and this time it looked like cards were disappearing up his sleeve. His discarded cards never made it to the pile with everyone else's, yet he still drew four new ones. She caught his tiny, relieved smile at the new cards before it vanished, too.

Both Merihim and Asmodeus stayed in until the end, but Kasyade won once more. Asmodeus threw his cards on the table, swearing, as he grabbed another beer, leaving Kasyade to deal again. "It's the cards," Asmodeus grumbled. "The deck likes Kas. Get the other one out, Merih. Maybe these cards will like me instead."

Merihim extracted another, identical pack of cards from his pocket and proceeded to shuffle them. "Are you in?" he asked Mel.

She took a deep breath and set her beer down on the table. "Sure. Why not?"

# Thirty-Four

Despite her protests, both Merihim and Asmodeus set a large pile of cash in front of her. "It's less than the coffee machine's worth," Merihim insisted, so Mel accepted it.

"Buy in," Kasyade grunted. Merihim and Asmodeus tossed in their fifty-dollar notes. Kasyade followed suit and they all stared at Mel.

"Oh, yes," she murmured, looking for a yellow note in her stack. She found one and placed it delicately on top of the other three in the middle of the table.

Kasyade shuffled the cards one more time and started dealing. First Merihim, then herself, before the other two got their cards. Round and round, until each had their five. Mel watched Asmodeus pick up each card he was dealt, one by one, and frown at it. Merihim waited for all five of his before grimacing at his hand.

Mel lifted her cards and fanned them out, pausing to rearrange them a little, before setting the fan back down on the table before her. "Remind me again," she said to no one in particular, "the aim of this game is to get as many of a kind as possible, with as high a number as I can, right?"

Kasyade and Asmodeus exchanged glances. Even Merihim looked startled, but he recovered first. "Pretty much, yeah. Unless you get all five in a sequence or of the same suit, but that doesn't happen often. It's easier to look for two or three or four of a kind, when you're just starting out."

Mel nodded and sipped her beer. "Thank you."

"Right, bets!" Kasyade announced, grinning.

"Merih?"

Merihim added five dollars to the pot and Mel followed his lead. Asmodeus shrugged before doing the same. Kasyade frowned and looked thoughtful but, after what seemed like an inordinately long amount of time, chose to place his purple five-dollar bill in the pot with the others.

"Right. How many cards you trading?" Kasyade said with his eyebrows raised.

"I'll go four," Merihim announced, throwing them down.

Kasyade swiped them up neatly and dealt him four fresh cards. Merihim's frown deepened as he looked at the cards, but he didn't say anything.

"Mel?"

"Mm?"

"How many cards are you trading? How many of the ones in your hand do you want to discard and replace with new ones?" Asmodeus asked patiently.

"Oh!" Mel peered at the backs of her cards, still face-down on the table. She looked thoughtful for a moment. "No, thank you. I'd like to keep these, if that's okay."

"All of them?" Asmodeus pressed. "Usually there's one or two, at least, and you could get a much better hand if you trade them in..."

Mel shook her head. "No, it really is okay. I'll keep the ones I have. It's a game of luck, right?" She smiled around the table.

Kasyade stared at her, mesmerised, as if he still didn't believe her. He had the look of a man who had just won a lot of money in a lottery, Mel decided. She shrugged. "Mo's next, right?"

Asmodeus had his two cards up, ready to trade. Kasyade's gaze swung to Asmodeus and he replaced the cards mechanically.

The other demons seemed intent on their own cards, so only Mel watched as Kasyade discarded one of his and dealt himself a new one. His big hands concealed his cards for a few seconds, and Mel wondered what he was trying to hide.

Kasyade seemed to notice her scrutiny and set his cards on the table, clapping his hands. "Right. Next round of betting. Merih?"

Merihim pouted at his cards, then pulled out

another five-dollar bill and surrendered it to the pot.

Mel hesitated. "I can match or make a larger bet, can't I?" she asked.

"Or fold," Kasyade added.

"Right." Mel nodded thoughtfully. She glanced at the piles of cash around the table. Kasyade seemed to have about as much as Asmodeus and Merihim put together, which was more than Mel had, too. "If I'm only playing one game, I could bet all of this, couldn't I?"

Three shocked pairs of eyes stared at her. Asmodeus attempted to smile. "You could, but it's usually safer to place smaller bets at first, until you get the hang of the game and the measure of your opponents..."

Mel smiled back. "You mean you all want to play cards with me again some time? When I'm not on such pressing business, of course. That would be lovely."

All three men nodded fervently, their gaze shifting to the money she was carefully transferring to the pot.

"I believe I'm all in?" she said.

"Y-yeah," Asmodeus stammered, throwing his cards down. "I can't match that. Fold."

Merihim dropped his cards, too. "Same."

Kasyade looked at Mel, who kept her serene smile firmly on her face. It was just a game to her, after all, and when it was over, she'd be able to pass through those gates and continue to Luce. The faster the game ended, the better. There definitely wasn't any point in drawing this out.

Kasyade opened his mouth.

Mel said, "Kas, you should probably fold, too. It would be in your best interests." She returned his gaze with concern.

Merihim coughed. "Mel, you shouldn't warn him if you have a good hand. Let him take the risk with his money and his hand — the point of the game is to win. You won't win if you tell people what you have in your hand. You could win some of our money back if you keep your cards a secret."

Mel tilted her head. "I don't understand. If Kas folds, I win. Isn't that the point?"

Merihim started to reply, but Kasyade cut him off. "But the point is, I don't fold, angel.

I'll not just match your bet – I'll raise you. I'll go all in, too. And you're out of cash." He grinned. "I'll take payment in other forms. Whatever you're offering."

Asmodeus and Merihim looked from Kasyade to Mel to their remaining funds. In unison, both men pushed their stacks toward Mel. "The rest of the coffee machine money, Mel," Asmodeus said.

Merihim nodded. "Yeah, I'll bet on you over my own hand any day. Match him."

Once again, Mel hesitated. "Are you sure, Kasyade?" she asked.

"Fold or match my bet, angel. Stop stalling," he replied.

She bowed her head. "I will match it." She counted out the money required and added it to the pot. What remained would barely buy lunch for the three of them on the Terrace.

Kasyade laughed. "Kiss my ass, angel. Four aces, look." He threw the hand down to reveal his cards to them all.

Asmodeus swore, but Merihim's jaw tightened. "What do you have, Mel?"

"I don't have four of a kind," she admitted.

"Actually, I don't have more than one of anything."

Kasyade laughed even harder. "You've got balls, angel – I never met one who could bluff like you before. I'll tell you what – I'll buy you a beer out of my winnings." He reached for the pot.

"NO!" The shout came from both Asmodeus and Merihim.

"I believe I have to show you my cards first," Mel stated. Her hands shaking a little, she turned over her fanned cards on the tabletop.

A hush fell.

"A royal flush," Merihim breathed.

"That's not possible!" Kasyade insisted. "I have all four aces. She must have been hiding the cards somewhere!"

Merihim looked from Mel to Kasyade. "Mel only touched those five cards, Kas, and she was naked when she arrived." He addressed Mel. "Where did you get the cards in your hand?"

"Kas dealt them to me," she replied.

"She's lying!" Kasyade declared.

"Angels don't lie," Asmodeus said slowly. "And they don't cheat, either. You've been cheating all night, you son of a harpy!" The table, money and cards went flying as Asmodeus dove for Kasyade. Kasyade got his arms up to shield his head, so all that got hurt was his sleeve, ripped up the seam to his elbow. Two more aces and a king fell out. "Forfeit! Forfeit all your winnings, you lying, cheating..."

Mel heard the smack of flesh on flesh, then bone breaking as Asmodeus and Kasyade hit the floor. She stood, hoping to help, but not sure how.

Merihim spread his arms. "You wanted to open the gate and go through, right? Now's probably a good time." He led her away from the wrestling demons. "How did you know he was cheating?"

Mel shrugged. "He had too many cards sometimes and some of them simply disappeared." She swallowed. "I gave him the opportunity to fold without having to show his hand, so he could make reparation to you both with his dignity intact, but he refused. I had hoped..."

Merihim snorted. "You're too innocent for your own good, Mel. We're demons. Damned, never to be redeemed."

Mel wished she could tell him that he was wrong, but perhaps Luce was unique among demons. He'd certainly been unusual enough to win her heart. "Call me an optimist, for I'll never lose hope," she murmured.

"Didn't you read the sign over the door? Hope deserts everyone here eventually," Merihim said.

Mel kept her smile soft. "Yet you hoped I'd win against Kas. You even bet money on the outcome."

Merihim coughed. "That's different. I've seen you win every gamble you take – when it's not for personal gain. Where did you learn to play poker?"

"France," Mel answered. When Merihim looked puzzled, she explained, "Poker was played in France before it arrived in New Orleans in America. Most people don't know that Napoleon's Russian retreat was because he lost a game of poker."

"I never heard that!" Merihim protested.

Mel smiled. "He had such an expressive face – he was terrible at bluffing. Given how well I knew him, I could read his hand simply from his expression."

Merihim's face registered his shock and Mel didn't wait for him to recover. "The gate?" she prompted. "I really need to see Luce."

Merihim heaved a huge sigh, shaking his head. "I hope you know what you're doing. Lord Lucifer is...well, he's in one of the darkest moods I've seen him in for centuries. You'd be better off going back to the surface. I'll give you a lift home, if you want."

"I must," Mel insisted. "I won't leave until I've seen him. Please open the gate."

Merihim coughed. "Actually, you have to be born an angel to do it. Just touch it – and it'll swing open. It works for us fallen angels, too, luckily, or we'd all be stuck on one side or the other. Not many angels make it this far without falling." He still looked regretful, Mel thought. "I don't want to see you fall. Even if you make it to Lucifer's lair, he'll do everything in his power to turn you, because he's a sadistic bastard. You don't deserve our fate, Mel. Turn back."

Mel placed both of her palms on the gates and they swung open, as if tonnes of stone were merely paper. She heard moans and screams from the depths below. She turned her head toward Merihim. "I can't turn back. Thank you for your help." She pulled his shirt over her head and handed it to him, before kissing his cheek.

Merihim took the shirt, stunned. "Any time, Mel. Mo and me...we owe you more than ever, now. Kas, too – I'll remind him that you gave him a chance to repent, when he wakes up and his arms grow back." He squinted at Asmodeus in the darkness. "Maybe before his arms grow back. I don't want him taking a swing at me, too." He blushed as he looked at Mel. "Lucifer will probably like what he sees, especially when he can see everything. I hope you reach him. Take care, Mel."

Mel smiled, waved, and stepped through the gates to the lower levels of Hell.

I'm coming for you, Luce, she thought, wishing he could hear her. Walking naked through Hell, just like you said in that café. I never thought it would be me doing it, though.

She stretched her wings and started her descent.

# Thirty-Five

Touching down on the first stone terrace, Mel was greeted by the grumpy receptionist she'd first met at her interview for the HELL Corporation. The girl had lost her clothes and gained a pair of dark, leathery wings, marking her as one of the Dirae, but Mel hadn't forgotten her frowning face.

"What do you want?" the girl asked, evidently appraising Mel's much larger wings.

Mel smiled and let her white wings fade from sight, wishing she had a way to wash some of the mud off the rest of her. "I'm looking for Lucifer. Do you have a switchboard, so you can call and tell him I'm here?"

The girl gave her a look of deep disgust. "No. Why would you...ohhh. You're that angel who wanted a job in the office up on the surface." She managed a nasty smile. "You come to try whoring yourself to Lord Lucifer for another chance? He has all the office whores he needs and the rest are all better looking than you. Maybe he'll find space for you with the harpies on Level Seven. Sometimes they run out of damned souls and they always need practice dummies."

Mel's smile didn't falter, though she wished she could increase the distance between herself and this nasty piece of work. Were all the demons in the lower levels as rude as this? Those in the upper levels had seemed so reasonable.

Mel cleared her throat. "I worked a long contract with the HELL Corporation on the surface. The work was very rewarding — fascinating, in fact. Now I've come to see Luce and I must admit, it's been interesting to see how he runs things in the Pit. What are those?" Mel nodded at several pits placed at regular intervals around the terrace – almost like open graves.

"Those?" The girl's grin became nastier still. "Part of the heating system for Level Seven. Want a closer look?" She gave Mel a shove toward the nearest one.

Sparks showered to the stone from where the girl had touched Mel, leaving scorch marks on her skin and the echo of the initial, painful burn. Mel found herself on her knees, but she rose as soon as the pain started to fade. A fading flash was all it was. Hardly enough to incapacitate an angel. The Dirae girl had disappeared.

Mel looked around. Perhaps the girl had fallen into one of the pits. She glanced into the nearest and saw what appeared to be a human figure, encased in flame as it lay on...was that molten rock? Pipes ran along the sides of the trench, with no markings to say what they contained. That meant they were filled with air or water, Mel knew. With a single thought, she split one of the pipes open. Water cascaded down the walls, rising as steam from the rock below. The pit began filling faster than the heat could evaporate it.

The extinguished but blackened figure disappeared in the cloud of steam, surfacing as the pit started to resemble a hot bath. "Thank you," a hoarse voice said. "They say I committed heresy, but I don't even know what religion they were from." As it rose from the warm water, Mel became aware that the burned heretic was most definitely male. "Oh, wait. They were Romans. I wouldn't give my wife to the slaves during the Saturnalia. Heresy, they called it. Unholy. Ha. My grandsire was a rabbi in Hieroselyma. Now he knew holy. Those crazy Romans..." His voice failed him at this point, to Mel's relief. She'd heard enough to know that this was a very strange level of Hell.

"Please, I was looking for the...girl responsible for this place," Mel said. "One of the Dirae, but I didn't catch her name. I think she might have fallen into one of these pits, but there are so many..."

He cleared his throat, coughed, then repeated the procedure. "Did you ask her name?"

Mel shook her head.

"Did you ever do anything to piss her off?"

"No, I met her on the surface, in an office. She was supposed to be helpful, but she seemed to begrudge even a moment of time to do her job and notify someone I was there to see..."

"Megaera, then. Alecto won't tell you her name and Tisiphone will fool you into thinking she's an angel until you cross her and then she'll rip you apart. Must've been Meg. She deserved a turn, burning in the pits." The man grinned with grim satisfaction. "She'll hurt for a bit, but she'll be fine again by morning. We always are, ready to be tortured all over again."

It was the second time she'd heard about the regeneration powers of Hell. Everything automatically healed by morning. So whatever was causing this silence from Luce should have healed by now, surely. How long had she been here? More than a day? Two? So hard to keep track of time when there was no daylight. She needed to find Luce. Find out why she couldn't even sense his soul.

Still, she could hardly leave the girl to burn. She had to help her first.

Mel ran along the line of pits, calling, "Meg. Megaera. Please, tell me where you are so I can help you out!"

The voice she heard was gravelly. "Bitch." It came from four pits down – she'd flown more than ten metres.

Mel increased her pace, splitting the pipes in all the pits open as she passed.

The dripping Dirae hauled herself out and glared at Mel. "I bet you did that on purpose." She ignored Mel's outstretched hand, clambering to her feet on her own. "Big joke from the bloody angel. I hope Lord Lucifer fucks you with his fork, if you even make it that far. Level Seven will just lap you up, I'm sure. A bit of fresh blood never hurt anybody...oh, except the angel shedding it, of course." Megaera pointed. "On to Level Seven and good riddance."

Mel tried to smile in the face of such malice. "Thank you."

As she left the girl behind, she heard the words, "With the pointy end, bitch."

Well, it was Hell. There had to be horrible people in it. Otherwise, why would the place exist at all? The shadows in the tunnel descending to Level Seven seemed darker than those above, but Mel assured herself she was just imagining it.

# Thirty-Six

The smell hit her first. The stench of old blood wafted up the tunnel, like the time Mel's neighbour had applied blood and bone fertiliser to her garden on a hot summer's day. Or the carnage at the Battle of Arausio, all over again. She wondered if the army commanders who led that slaughter were here among the damned. It seemed fitting for such mass murderers to bathe in a boiling river of blood just like the one before her.

She couldn't tell one struggling figure apart

from the others — they all seemed to be submerged in the gruesome ooze.

"You're far from home, angel. Want a ride somewhere?"

Mel tore her eyes from the river. She hadn't seen a centaur in years, and this one was leering at her. Combing her memory, she found his name — Nessos, the ferryman who liked to rape his female passengers. "No, thank you. Directions to Lucifer's lair are all that I ask."

"Lord Lucifer?" Nessos scoffed. "He can't fill you like I can. Even humans know that — they say a well-endowed man is hung like a horse, not like Lucifer. If you're looking for some action, demon style, you won't find a rougher rider than me. I can make you scream, angel, so they'll hear you in Heaven."

Mel managed a polite smile. "Tempting, I'm sure, but I need to speak to Lucifer. I take it I'll have to cross the river?"

"And the bank on the other side. You do like it rough, then, if you're headed into the harpies' territory." Nessos stared at her, seemingly impressed. "You're braver than me.

I'll just fuck you — those girls will fuck you up."

Struggling not to show her disgust, Mel forced herself to maintain her strained smile as she flapped her wings, trying to rapidly rise above the depraved centaur.

Her shadow darkened the river's sluggish surface, but it seemed to gather density as it lost form. It looked like a dark cloud beneath her, keeping pace with her progress as she trudged deeper into Hell for Luce.

Luce.

Mel reached out for his soul, straining for a sense of him that she couldn't grasp. He seemed so distant she couldn't feel him at all. Had he left Hell while she struggled to make it through to him? That would be the ultimate irony — if he'd left Hell to look for her. Surely Michael and Peter would tell him where she was — even Raphael, for Michael must have told him everything by now. If she reached Luce's lair before he returned, she was claiming his throne while she waited or, better yet, his bed. She couldn't recall ever being so weary on Earth. She longed for rest — but she couldn't stop yet. Luce needed her — that much she knew.

She touched down on the rocky ledge that hung over the river – too high for those poor, drowning souls to grasp, but just high enough for a centaur to poke his spear at anyone who made the attempt.

"I said no! The harpies don't need any more assistants. Only volunteers to be victims and Jez said she doesn't want to see your arse again. Get down!" Chiron the centaur jabbed at a gory figure, who subsided into the red river. "You should fly right back where you came from," Chiron said, leaning on the spear as he squinted at Mel. "There's nothing but pain if you go any further."

Mel smiled wanly. "My feet already hurt and it seems all the foot spas in Hell are broken. I carry my pain with me and the sooner I see Lucifer, the sooner I can head home for a rest."

"No angel should see what the harpies are up to. I'm not even game to go in there. The screams are enough." The centaur shuddered, from his human shoulders right down to his equine tail.

"Is there another way through to Lucifer's lair?"

Chiron shook his head. "Few make it through and they say he won't see anyone. You're wasting your time."

Mel's heart twinged as she wondered if he was right. Perhaps she should just turn around and return home. Luce knew where she lived – if he wanted her, he could find her.

But if he was hurt and needed her help...

"No. My time is never wasted, though there are some things I wish I hadn't seen. I'm sure it won't be as bad as you say – I've worked with some of the harpies up on the surface. This is Lilith's domain, and she and I get along just fine." Mel bowed her head. "Thank you, but I will continue, as I must. If you see Lucifer..." She wasn't sure what to ask for.

Chiron bowed deeply. "In the unlikely event that I see Lord Lucifer, I'll say that you seek him and that he is undoubtedly in your debt. You should have summoned him to the surface and not endured such hardship." A vaguely humanoid figure surged up from the revolting river. "OI! I said no!" Chiron levelled his spear at the offending soul. "Get back in there or I'll..."

His voice faded as Mel entered the next cave and the chorus of screams drowned out all other sounds. There was so much suffering here.

# Thirty-Seven

To Mel's surprise, the new cave was a maze of tall partitions, reminiscent of the HELL Corporation offices. The ruddy, flickering light made this scene far more eerie – especially with the screaming. She tucked her wings out of sight, so they wouldn't catch on anything in the narrow passage.

Mel peered around the first partition and wished she hadn't. Light caught the metal barbs on a many-tailed whip as it swished through the air to embed itself in the torn flesh that had once been a damned soul's back. This soul gave a hoarse groan, as if his voice had fled long since. The whip-wielder yanked her weapon free, pulling flesh and blood with it.

Mel edged away, trying not to gag. She wanted to close her eyes and run right back up to the surface. This was Hell and for her, it was true torture.

She quickened her steps, trying to be silent. She couldn't leave this level soon enough for her liking. As for looking into any of the other cubicles...she wasn't sure she could face it.

A gurgling scream broke her resolve and Mel's eyes darted toward the sound. The sizzle and stench of searing flesh hit her as she realised this demon's weapon of choice was a branding iron. No, a whole collection of the things — she saw the bundle of metal rods protruding from the fire. The soul writhed on the table, pinned there by the demon's weight.

"Oh, yes, baby. Do that again," Jezebeth's voice cooed as she shifted to seize another brand. Glowing metal met flesh and the man bucked beneath her. She rode him with a moan of pleasure.

Surely no one could enjoy others' pain so much that they craved sex while inflicting it.

Jezebeth let out a triumphant shriek. Evidently she did.

Mel hastened away, but not quickly enough to miss Jezebeth's voice saying, "One more orgasm like that, baby, and I'll let you come, too."

Bile rose in Mel's throat and she fell to her knees, retching. The smells, the sounds and the sheer horror of it all were too much for her. Oh Hell, she had to get out of here. Luce. She had to find Luce.

"One trying to escape? Oh, no, pretty one. I've got a special new steel strap-on I'd like to try out on you. I sharpened it 'specially this morning. Don't worry, your impaled insides will heal again tomorrow. The big question is, which hole do I fuck first?" Like Jezebeth's voice, this one was familiar, but Mel didn't have time to place it.

Claws dug deep into Mel's back, grating on bone, and Mel heard her own screaming. More pain burned and the sharp talons were torn away, taking flesh with them. Mel swallowed carefully before she dared to look at the wound. Her attacker had sheared her shoulder down to the bone, but the blast of their souls touching had cauterised it so the wound wasn't bleeding. There was a chunk of flesh missing from her back and her attacker couldn't be far away.

Mel clambered to her feet, searching the space for her assailant. Ananiel lay sprawled against one wall, like a thrown doll. Her manic grin disturbed Mel deeply and that was before she saw the demon's hands.

Ananiel sniffed her gory fingers with relish. "Mmm, angel meat. Good thing it's not long 'til morning. I'll take burns and a broken back for an hour or so to taste meat this sweet." She poked two fingers into her mouth, noisily sucking the flesh from them.

Revolted, Mel couldn't think of a fitting reply.

She was saved by Ananiel's violent coughing fit. "Fuck, that's too sweet!" Ananiel choked out. "It's like super-concentrated sugar at boiling point!" Her black tongue sent up wisps of smoke as she tried to spit out her mouthful of Mel. "Oh, it burns, it burns!"

"I don't advise you do that again," Mel said.

"Fuck, no," Ananiel spat. "Angel meat's barely fit for dog food. I should've carved you up to serve you to Cerberus."

Mel smiled for the first time since entering this charnel cave. "I've already fed Cerberus. He preferred pork sausages."

"Ana, you're supposed to be bringing the new souls to me, not playing with them in the corridor." Lilith appeared, her breasts bursting out the top of her black leather corset, which was all the clothing she wore. Mel stared at her former boss, reflecting that demons didn't need to wax, as there wasn't a single hair evident from Lilith's breasts down to her black stilettos. Lilith returned Mel's stare until the blushing angel focussed her eyes firmly on the shiny shoes. "What the Hell are you doing here?" Lilith asked.

"I'm here to see Luce."

Lilith snorted. "The big baby's not seeing anyone. Apparently, one of your angels pulled some sort of trick on him and he's sulking in his office." She eyed Mel with a calculated air.

"You might be exactly what the devil ordered to cheer him up. Gerry!" she shouted over her shoulder.

Sounding like a large bat, Geryon's leathery wings flapped at the end of the corridor. "I'm not dragging any more souls out of the bloody river for you today, Lili. Jez is due to finish up for the day and she promised we'd spend the evening together. I'm going to wear my...what's Mel doing here?"

"She's here to see Lord Lucifer, apparently. I need you to escort her safely through to his lair. Wouldn't want anything to happen to her on her way to see the boss, would we? He likes his angels as pristine as possible," Lilith purred.

Geryon looked torn. "But Jez..."

"Will be waiting for you when you get back. I'll tell her how eager you are," promised Lilith.

He bowed, gesturing for Mel to go first. "Let's get you to your destination. I'm sure we both have better places to be than the harpies' little club. I don't know about you, but once the blades come out and they start hacking bits off, I always wish armour was still in vogue."

# Thirty-Eight

Geryon led the way into a steep, twisting passage. Mel counted three turns before he held his hands up for a halt. "Please," he said. "I want to ask you a favour. I know I have no right to ask and I'm a demon, so you have no reason to trust me. I want you to close your eyes. Your ears. Your whole mind. As you travel through this place, I don't want you to judge me by my job here. This is the worst level of Hell, where even the imps won't come. The souls here are damned for the most heinous crimes and their punishment persists for eternity, in the hope that they might feel some portion of the pain they've caused in their lifetimes. Even Lord Lucifer hates this level — it's where he sends demons for punishment. You're such a sweet angel. I don't want you scarred by what you see here."

Mel was touched. Geryon couldn't know what atrocities she'd seen humans commit — perhaps even some of the very souls entrusted to his...attentions. It was sweet of him to want to protect her. Yet he was a demon and she knew she couldn't trust him.

"I need to reach Luce," she said. "Is there another way to get to him, without walking through this horrible layer of Hell?"

He shook his head. "No. I'll guide you, Mel — every step of the way. Just close your eyes and trust me. Or...or leave. I can guide you all the way to the surface and home. Make an appointment to see him at the office. Mephi will set you up." His eyes looked hurt, she thought.

Looking deep into the demon's eyes, she tried to read his soul. Darkness swirled...and seemed to reach for her. Sighing, Mel retreated. Luce was the only denizen of Hell she trusted, for his was the only soul she could read. "I'm sorry, Gerry, but you won't be able to lead me through without touching me if I'm closing my eyes and ears to everything here. You know you can't do that without getting hurt. If you lead me through as quickly as possible, I'll do my best not to...not to look. This is Hell and you're just doing your job, right?"

Geryon looked hesitant. "I was going to offer to carry you. Fly you over the worst of it and down to the next level. It's how I manage to get through my work day. If you could fly, it wouldn't be a problem..."

His mouth dropped open as Mel unfolded her feathers. Her clawed shoulder ached, but no more so than before. She swung her wings in a powerful beat, rising as only an angel could. "Lead the way."

Leathery wings flapped furiously as Geryon struggled to reach Mel's altitude. "All right. Follow me and don't look down. Even from above, some of the torture bolgies are disturbing. We had to separate them into bolgies or the damned souls complained that other crimes had lesser punishments than theirs. I hate to say it, but I'll take an eternity of screaming over arrogant whining any day."

The demon flew as erratically as a black cockatoo, Mel mused as she glided after him. Strange smells assailed her nostrils – raw sewage, the acrid fumes from boiling pitch, the stench of burning flesh and the underlying notes of spilled blood. She caught a glimpse of flame out of the corner of her eye and directed her gaze at what appeared to be a ditch full of fire, the shadowy forms of damned souls writhing as they burned. Souls burning for eternity – this was the picture she'd had of Hell, repeated incessantly in human media over millennia. Yet it represented one tiny trench amid all the horrors Hell had to offer. A great, dark cloud seemed to obscure all of the sections of this level, as if the flames generated more smoke than Mel thought possible. Yet this cloud looked alive, roiling like a storm and weaving like a snake searching for prey. Hell, it looked like it was staring at her, trying to decide if she'd do for dinner, as it slowly rose for a closer look. Sentient smoke? Oh, how silly. Maybe she really was tired and she should rest.

"Don't look down!" Geryon shouted, and Mel focussed on riding the updraft away from the source of hot air and the curious cloud.

Geryon dived, heading for a black hole in the cavern floor. As they dropped, so did the temperature; goosebumps broke out all over Mel's body. While the air temperature plummeted, their descent remained steady until Geryon touched down on the stony floor of a huge cavern.

Mel's natural glow barely lit any of it, leaving many dark, shadowy corners. She felt surrounded by ominous malice, but she couldn't pinpoint the source. Her feet touched stone so cold that she cried out. It wasn't stone at all, but dirt-encrusted ice. This portion of Hell had frozen over and the air was positively frigid.

"Welcome to Level Nine," Geryon said, gesturing. "The damned souls here are fewer in number, but they're far worse than those in my level. Frozen forever in the lowest layer of Hell, so they won't hurt anyone else, and guarded by Lord Lucifer himself. Most demons never come this deep into Hell unless Lord Lucifer summons them. As for angels...I don't know any who've ever made it this far." He paused. "Do you think you'll be all right on your own? Jez is about to knock off work and I've got her favourite flogger all ready. If I hurry, I might even have time to slip into my mankini..."

Mel smiled and wished him a pleasant evening – not that she thought any evening involving flogging and the mankini she remembered all too well could be pleasant, but each to their own. Perhaps demons enjoyed inflicting pain on one another while they wore hideous, skimpy clothing. Who was she to judge? They were certainly consenting adults, after all.

She watched Geryon spiral upward, wondering at what seemed to be thickening shadows pouring over the lip of the pit and into the cavern where she stood. Ah, it was only smoke. Mel had more on her mind than the fumes of Hell. She needed to find Luce — he had to be on this level. How could he hide himself from her?

# Thirty-Nine

"Have you been torturing the damned in here? You should get someone to clean up – ugh, you should get cleaned up. What possessed you to sleep in a pool of congealing blood? Have you been watching vampire movies again, Luce?"

Darkness, but there'd been Mel. She'd come to comfort him, but she couldn't stay. She'd had a pressing task, someone she'd had to save, and he'd floated in the dark, hoping and waiting for her to return, but she hadn't. It had seemed so real...

Luce lifted his head. There was blood all over the floor and he had a Hell of a headache. He didn't remember torturing anyone...he had agony enough to fell an army, and he...damn. Demons couldn't die after all – and demonic weapons couldn't kill him. Maybe somewhere, that meant Mel was alive, too. He had to hope. Even if he never saw her again, at least he'd know she lived.

"What's up with you and all the extra security? I had to shove through some sort of energy shield to get through here – the static frizzed my hair up something awful. Not as bad as you, though. You look like Hell – no pun intended, because you look worse than this gloomy place. What happened? Did Mel leave you?" Persephone's perky voice grated on his grief. She laughed – deeper and darker than her usual giggle. "You know an angel of her rank wouldn't stay long with someone like you."

Luce lifted his head to glare. He had nothing to say to her.

She perched on the corner of his desk,

swinging her leg beneath her long skirt. "I had to attend the Minister's dinner in your stead. He was quite attentive – wanted to give the corporation advance warning of some of the new contracts on the horizon. Privatising the ports under one company...and Lili's very eager about the possibility of winning the Department for Child Protection contract, too. Anything I should know about Lili?" She gave a wicked little smile. "Oh, and I donated all your reserve red wines to a charity auction for the children's hospital, in the company's name, of course. Raised our profile plenty – and now I have that space for my china doll collection. So many pretty porcelain faces, instead of those dusty, dreary bottles..." She prattled on, not seeming to notice that Luce wasn't listening any more.

He'd have shared the wine with Mel happily, but now he didn't care what happened to it. He dropped his forehead to the sticky stone, wishing she'd go away and leave him to his misery.

It took a while for him to realise, but it hit him like a brick when it did: here, he was still the Lord of Hell. He could make her leave.

"Get out," he growled, shoving with all the supernatural forces he could muster to send her back to the surface and out of his domain.

She giggled. "You gave me all your power — everything. You can't order me around in this place — you made me your equal." She lifted her hand eagerly, looking like a naughty child about to steal the moon.

Luce felt the power of her push, but he resisted it. "Not my equal," he grunted. "More like second in charge, when I'm absent. I'm still the lord of this place. Now get out."

"Aww, don't sulk," she simpered. "I came to offer you some solace. You can do anything you like to me, honest. No strings attached." She held up the strings that had tied her dress around her neck, showing him that if she dropped them, the whole outfit would fall to the floor.

The ink on her thighs, glorifying Hell as if it was worth putting permanently on her skin. Ah, Hell — it was like tattooing a blocked toilet on her backside to entice a plumber.

Luce looked. He wondered if he'd ever have

been able to summon up some enthusiasm for the young woman who was so willing to bare everything before him. Before he'd met Mel.

He'd never know. After Mel, he felt nothing any more. Not for Persephone; not for anyone.

"I'd rather have Mel's rotting corpse than you. I said get out. Mel's gone. Let me mourn her in peace," he snapped, pointing at the door.

Persephone bristled, tying her dress again with shaking hands. "You're one delusional demon if you believe Mel would ever have any feelings for you."

"She said she loved me," Luce whispered, regretting it the moment he said it.

"And you think that makes you special?" Persephone sneered. "Mel loves everyone. It's just the sort of angel she is."

For a moment, he believed her. The sheer horror that he'd imagined Mel's love...

BULLSHIT.

Mel didn't lie. Not with words, expression or body language. She'd loved him – even as he killed her. She hadn't looked at anyone else the way she had at him.

He rose onto his elbows. "Get out. I won't tell you again. If you think your power matches mine, I'll call in every demon and devil under my command and we'll see who they obey. I'll have them drag you out by your hair – across all the circles of Hell to the gate. And when they dump you outside in the hot desert sands, I'll laugh. I never want to hear another word from you about Mel – and I definitely don't want to see you again."

She lifted her little nose in the air. "You can keep everyone else out, but not me, Luce. Remember that." And with that, she disappeared.

He wanted to follow her and choke the life out of her, but he didn't want to hear any more of her lies. He might not be powerful enough to kill her – he might have conceded too much of his personal power to her in his hope for Mel. Like all hopes in Hell, any chance he'd had with Mel was long gone now – fled far from here.

Stiffly, he rose to his feet and surveyed the mess. The amount of blood looked like he'd slaughtered a pig, or at least butchered several damned souls, instead of attempting suicide. He stared at his wrists, but the holes had closed and healed as if they'd never been. He'd made a Hell of a mess of the floor and his clothes. His fork still had flesh clinging to the barbs – enough to make him feel sick, even though he knew it was only pieces of him.

How did suicide victims' families clean up after a crime like this? Losing a loved one and having to clean up the mess afterwards? Fury ripped through him. The harpies were hardly punishment enough for them – he was going to make them clean the torture chambers on Level Eight. With tiny toothbrushes and no gloves. Let them deal with blood and severed limbs, the smells and sounds of torture echoing around them every day. It was nothing compared to what they'd put people through in their selfishness, violence and waste as they ended the precious gift of their own lives... Demons couldn't die, but he'd damn well make every suicide sinner wish they could, all over again.

But first, he had to clean up his own mess,

or the senior demons would know he hadn't been torturing anyone in here but himself. And the Lord of Hell could never show weakness to a demon, because they knew how to take advantage of that...

Luce summoned a bucket and a scrubbing brush, detergent and hot water. This job required hard work and he couldn't trust anyone but himself to do it. He cleaned up his own messes, damn it, and he wouldn't make the same mistake again.

Right after he'd had a hot shower, he was going to find out what had gone on in Hell in his absence. If the interfering angel who'd made a mockery of the gates and his grief had returned, he'd know about it. He decided to start with the weakest one first.

# Forty

Mel lost count of the number of times she'd slipped on the gritty ice. At least the limestone dust was white and not black, so she looked like she'd been rolled in flour or sugar, like some sort of scone. How long had it been since she'd eaten something? Hot, fresh scones sounded wonderful, with whatever she could lay her hands on. Butter. Jam and cream. Jarrah honey. A fresh-brewed cup of tea.

As soon as she reached home, she'd do some baking. A trip to the shop for ingredients and an afternoon of domestic bliss, showering her kitchen in flour as she cooked up a storm. Maybe even with Luce, if she could drag him out of this horrible place. Wearily, she reached for his soul, praying that this time she'd sense him again, though she'd been disappointed so many times since she entered Hell that she wasn't sure what to hope for any more.

Misery. Pain. Anger. Frustration that blood was impossible to clean off porous white surfaces. Deep desire for her...

LUCE! Mel stumbled and fell, but she barely felt the pain. She'd found his soul again and he was close. All she had to do was find him.

Rising laboriously to her knees, she closed her eyes and sent her thoughts searching for him once more. A cold gust of wind chilled her to the bone, but she persisted. He was here.

Luce was...somewhere near the source of the freezing breeze, it seemed. She felt him most strongly when she faced into the frigid air current. Opening her eyes, Mel peered into the darkness, seeing only the dark cavern wall. Her eyes moved down and she caught a glimmer of light, through an opening close to the ground. She'd have to crawl through it, but if it led to Luce...it wasn't as if she had any pride to lose. Losing Luce when she was so close would be a far worse fate.

Prostrate, she slid across the ice onto sand. Tears of relief tracked down her cheeks as she pulled her body through the narrow tunnel, wondering if this was what snakes felt like. No, snakes couldn't cry. Nor could they feel the sort of love bursting out of her soul as she sensed the object of it was so close. Oh God, what if she'd given up and left him here to his fate?

The tunnel widened, the walls disappearing into the darkness, and Mel clambered stiffly to her feet, brushing dust off her body. She could see a faint light in the distance, so that's where she directed her weary steps.

# Forty–One

"I've had no report from you all week. How are the damned doing on Level Four?" Luce asked.

Ploutos gave a shaky shrug. "Same. They battle pointlessly and the cats play. I took a video of the cats playing and Nybbas uploaded it onto the humans' internet in the office. He called it Cats from Hell and it went viral, he said, which is good. Spreading like some sort of horrible disease among humans. I recorded a few more and he's looking to put in subliminal messages, like 'Greed is good' and 'You need sex now but you don't need to know his name' and 'HELL Corporation is your hero'. All standard propaganda, he said."

Luce stared at him. "Cat videos? Humans can get sick from cat videos?"

"No, Lord Lucifer. Nybbas said it's a sort of sickness of the mind. He said it makes them forget everything else and want more cat videos. They flood the internet with such things. He said it inspires sloth, laziness, procrastination...all things that bring people to us." Ploutos' face moved in a fleeting smile, as if there was more he wanted to say, but wouldn't.

"So there's no change in your domain?" Luce pushed. "No unusual visitors, or anything strange happening?"

Ploutos screwed his face up. "Mmm...mmmy sister came to visit," he managed to say.

"Your sister?"

"My sister...Persephone. She...she comes to visit and asks questions about you, Lord Lucifer. I believe you have a very willing recruit there, if you're looking for junior demons."

"Oh Hell, no! That's the last thing I need – that little nephilim permanently here in Hell. I can't imagine anything worse. I don't want her anywhere near here again, you hear? You go visit her on the surface – every weekend, if you want, but I don't want to see her in Hell." Luce looked down at his list. "Go tell Camael and Samael I need to see them."

"That's all you wanted to know?" Ploutos asked, looking almost happy.

Luce stared at the small man. "Is there anything else I need to know that you should be telling me?"

"Ah...ah...no, Lord Lucifer," Ploutos mumbled. "I'll go get the twins. And then...more cat videos!"

Cat videos. Humans were crazy, Luce decided, and Ploutos wasn't far behind. But if he was related to Persephone, he wasn't surprised.

Camael and Samael, he thought. The experts in animal welfare. He had a job for them.

# Forty-Two

Mel crossed the cold cavern and found an ordinary door, set in a fairly standard door frame in the rock. The icy blast blew from this open doorway. She didn't need directions or a map. She knew Luce lay through this portal.

She stepped inside, face turned toward the full-bore fan from the air conditioner as it blew a fine mist of dust from her hair. Now she wished she'd brought the tablecloth from Heaven, or, better yet, a coat. But...no. She'd come this far without anything. Her clothes were inside this room and she'd have them back soon enough.

"I don't want to hear any more excuses," she heard Luce's voice state without emotion. "I want to know the dog is fed, twice daily, as he should be. We have a reputation to maintain and that includes animal welfare. I've taken Kas off animal control and I'm making both of you responsible for Cerberus – a hungry dog has questionable loyalty and he's a guard dog, after all. There's always space in the lower levels of Hell for more souls if you feel this is beneath you."

Mel heard sullen voices murmuring their acquiescence. With a degree of pleasure, she noticed it was Camael and Samael, the two former angels who'd coined the animal welfare legislation that had caused so much trouble for herself and Gabrielle in the office. Karma was indeed a bitch – one who liked dogs.

Luce dismissed the fallen angels and Mel stepped back against the concrete wall to let them exit. Both nodded to her in recognition before leaving quickly. Samael shut the door behind him.

She took a deep breath, letting it leave her before she rounded the corner to where she could see Luce. He sat at the desk, his head buried in his hands. He didn't seem to be aware of her presence.

This close, she could tell the darkness he surrounded himself with was guilt. She could feel it rolling off him in waves. The soul within, though despairing, was as light as ever. The dark master of Hell no longer had the heart for the job. She wanted to reach out to him, to comfort him, but she didn't know what to say.

As Mel hesitated, Luce looked up and his eyes met hers. His face was flat, revealing nothing. "A very well-thought out illusion, but not very thorough," he said after some time. She could feel her heart close to breaking at the pain in his, but he showed no outward sign of it at all. He stood and approached her. "You see, you've missed details. The real Mel had a scar on her index finger from a fight with a stapler. She had a half-healed burn on her hand from where she spilled her tea when I surprised her in the kitchen last week. And she had two gaping holes here." Luce pointed at her breasts, making Mel wish they didn't stand out so prominently in the cold air. His eyes were hard as he looked at her. "She'd also be perfectly presentable and clothed, without a hair out of place. You have mud splatters up to your thighs and limestone dust everywhere. Nice try, but you can get out." This time he pointed at the door.

Mel blinked. "I wasn't focussing on blemishes when I assembled this body. They weren't necessary. I've just crossed the nine circles of Hell, looking for you. I felt you were more important than a few streaks of mud or the dust accumulating outside your front door that I had to crawl through to get here, though I'd love a shower if you can point me the way to your bathroom. Mud sure sticks in this place – especially from that swampy River Styx."

Luce laughed. "No angel's ever made it through all the circles of Hell. They give in to despair, or corruption, or disgust at the array of sins the souls here have committed. You're a demon in disguise, though a good disguise. Did Persephone put you up to this to distract me?"

"I'll certainly be paying Persi a visit when we get out of here, but I haven't spoken to her yet. I wanted to see you first," Mel said, allowing a little of her irritation to colour her tone. Some demons were dense, but today Luce really took the cake. Surely he knew her better than that. "You do know that angels aren't capable of deception, don't you?"

"Which is why you must be a demon, not some decoy sent by those bastards in Heaven," Luce replied bitterly.

"Leave here with me and I'll show you, Luce. I don't want to drag you out of here against your will and I haven't come this far, only to leave alone. I want you to choose to come with me."

"I told you to get out and you will." He waved at the door and Mel felt the full force of his will, pushing her in the direction of the exit. It wafted right past her, though — his power was in no way equal to hers. Even here.

Patiently, she stood her ground and held his gaze.

Luce's eyes widened in surprise.

"Persephone? Now you've given yourself away. No one else in Hell has that kind of power. Appearing in Mel's body... This is beyond a joke. You have everything you asked for. Leave me to my solitude." He walked back to the desk and threw himself into the chair, his eyes staring at the concrete wall.

Mel wasn't sure if she wanted to laugh or cry. How could Luce forget that angels couldn't die? She could feel his grief and guilt, yet he couldn't accept that she was herself.

"Please leave," Luce said again, his voice cracking. Mel could see tears brimming in his eyes as his hand tightened on a bundle of white cloth in his lap. "Please. If there is any sympathy, any kindness left in you at all, I'm asking you to leave. I don't want to see you here again."

Mel reached out. "Luce." If she could touch him, she'd know why he wanted to shut her out. Maybe she'd even know what to say. While she'd been wandering through Hell, what had happened to him? What had Persi done?

He yanked his arms back, as if shielding his

heart with them. "Don't touch me. Just get out. Now."

Wordlessly, she turned her back on him and marched toward the door. She didn't want him to see her cry for him. She'd come too late to help. All this had been for nothing and Luce didn't deserve her failure.

# Forty-Three

Tears blurred her eyes as shadows surrounded her. The darkest shadows she'd only glimpsed as she strode through Hell now seemed to have congregated here, lying in wait. Like the shadows she'd first seen on Luce's soul, which he'd somehow sold to Persephone for her. Or the sort that had hidden him from her as she walked through the deeper levels of Hell. The sentient cloud she thought she'd glimpsed on Level Eight didn't seem so silly now.

Her eyes flew to the open door behind her,

which was darkening already as if beset by black smoke. But there was no fire – this smoke was made from souls. The blackest souls this world had ever known. So dark they couldn't be confined to a single circle of Hell, for its punishments and tortures held no power over them any more. She could feel the malice pouring off them – they had neither name nor identity. They were clouds of hate. And they were headed for Luce's lair, to hurt him more than she already had. To Hell with that.

She shouted, sealing off the entrance even as they deserted the door to attack her. It had been centuries since she'd fought anything stronger than a ladle-jammed drawer – or used a weapon other than words. But today she fought for one she loved. One she'd wronged and owed reparation to, who had begged for her help. Nothing could withstand a righteous angel, and she had a millennia-old wrong to right.

She breathed deep and steady, feeling the malice swirling around her. Closing in. The shadows whispered of failure, of pain, of the day humans stoned her to death for daring to make a difference in Crete so many millennia ago. Angels in Hell would fall because nothing was stronger than they. Not even the Lord of Hell could destroy them, for this was their domain, before it ever was his. Growing in strength through the ages until nothing could match them. They would destroy him.

Mel was painfully reminded of the memory Luce had shared with her before they'd left for Heaven. His fall and the shadows closing in. Not metaphorical shadows, she realised, but these – those that had surrounded his soul and pushed for a way in. A way they hadn't found yet, no matter how hard they'd fought.

The hissing whispers told her what they wished to do. First, they'd destroy the arrogant angel who thought she was better than them, that she could best them with her petty perfection.

"Not your domain. Your prison. I am not perfect and I never will be, but each day I strive to be better and that lies at the heart of an angel." She kept her voice steady.

Weakening in the world, with every step

through Hell, the shadows continued. Another angel would fall. Couldn't match their strength. They'd been watching. Still wounded from the harpy. Too weak to fight.

Mel's arms ached from how tightly she held her knees to her chest, crouching on the floor. She'd hold firm and protect herself until they gave up.

Stupid angel to think she could take on Hell. Too weak. Too arrogant. She would fail. Here, they were strongest. She was no match for them. They would never give up, the shadows insisted.

"Nothing can match you in here, but Hell is tiny compared to the world I walk in. The powerful have no need to enter here. You can never leave to see. Never..." She cried for the once-damned souls, driven to madness in this confined space with no chance of redemption, until they became nothing but malicious whispers and intent. The shadows crowded closer to her, as if they would drink her tears. "Take them," she said, flinging her arms wide. "Drink my pity for you."

The hissing continued, No pity for the weak

angel. No one would come to help her. She would fall and one day join them. All souls did.

Mel's mouth flew open at the thought of souls that didn't even know of the presence of Heaven, or anything outside this dark cave. And they never would. A dark tendril of shadow, almost like a finger, touched the tear on her cheek. She couldn't see the door to Luce's lair, they shrouded her so thickly, but Mel could see the tendrils forming what looked like a hand. She reached out and grasped it.

That one touch let her read the entire swirling cloud of souls. A miasma...many minds with no recollection of who they once were, but burning with desire...all wanting one thing. To get out and wreak havoc on Earth again, on those who had trapped them here. If they tormented Luce enough, he might send them away far enough to escape...but first, they would imprison this angel's soul like they had everyone else's — starting with the one she'd come to save. Mel watched them remember shrouding Luce the first time he'd fallen into Hell from Heaven — the angel thrown among them — even as he'd tried to shut them out.

That's what angels did. They curled in on themselves, tried to protect themselves from darkness as it surrounded them and won. By the time they realised, it was too late – their soul was sealed in with no escape. No angel was brave enough to burn – not after they'd seen the other burning souls in Hell.

Souls fell, but the source of the taint was here. Mel wasn't going to let them surround another soul. Even if she had to surrender her own to destroy them. If they touched her soul, they'd burn with her. Maybe she could light a pyre that even Luce, the hot devil, would notice.

Poor, naked angel. No clothes, no help, no pity. Only tears. Like the day they stoned her to death. She could relive that here. Over and over and over again. Just like the Lord of Hell, remembering the day he killed her. Or his fall from Heaven.

"NO!" She could take her own pain. She knew her failings and her failures. Luce didn't deserve guilt for what she knew was her fault. Hadn't she come this far? To Hell with hiding what she really was – Hell's fires only consumed bodies, but as an angel, she could destroy souls. If the shadows really wanted her, they'd need to be stronger than they thought possible.

Mel shot to her feet. The weight of her wings tugged at her shoulders, but she stood firm. Her soul burned for justice denied and nothing could withstand a righteous angel. It was time for her to show her light. "You will not touch him. You won't touch any angel, demon or the Lord of Hell. Not even the damned, unless they approach you directly. I forbid it." The cave seemed brighter, and the shadows became more insubstantial. She could barely see the tendril fingers she still held in hers. "If you want my soul, take it!"

Her spirit swelled like a supernova, enveloping the cloud and lapping the very walls of the cavern. She could feel them all and they burned. She burned with them, but it was worth the pain. A hundred times worse than the energy surge she'd felt when Merihim had first touched her; ten times worse than the burn that had defended her from Ananiel and the Dirae's attacks, but never more than she could bear. She was stronger than any dark, malicious soul that could only prey on the weak.

"Time weakened you and so it will continue until you are no more! Do not enter my sight again." She pointed at the entrance tunnel to Level Nine and watched as a beam from her fingertip hit the wall with a splash of light. What was left of the shadows seemed like a tiny curl of smoke, rapidly eddying away from her.

The smack of flesh on flesh reverberated through the cave, startling her. Mel heard it again before she whirled around, looking for the source.

Luce leaned against the doorway to his lair, slowly clapping. He still held her clothes in the crook of one arm.

Why hadn't he come to her aid, or even attempted to call off the fiendish souls? Not that she'd needed his help, but it was the principle. Hadn't he cared that she was in danger?

Or had he lured her here, knowing what lurked in the shadows, hoping their dark malice could corrupt her when he couldn't? Was that why he'd stood back – to watch? Maybe the imps weren't the only voyeurs in this place.

She hadn't journeyed naked through Hell to be anyone's entertainment. She'd come to save him. If he didn't want her help, she was done with him.

"You." Luce's startled eyes met hers. "Give me back my underwear," she commanded, striding forward.

# Forty-Four

Persephone couldn't...surely she couldn't have done that. She wasn't as strong as he was – and he was no match for those souls. Suddenly, he felt the need to go back to his desk, where he could put a block of solid timber between himself and this angel gone nova. Not daring to take his eyes off her, he backed away. It couldn't be. But if it was...

She passed through the energy barrier as if it didn't exist – the same barrier he'd been trapped behind – and her relentless steps carried her closer to him.

Her wings grazed the doorway, but she didn't stop to fold them back. "I've walked naked through to the very inner circle of Hell and I'll be damned before I leave empty-handed. If you're not coming with me like I thought you would, I can at the very least leave with the clothes you stole from me. You can keep the shirt if you wish, but if you're going to pretend I'm dead or call me by another woman's name, I draw the line at my underwear. I want it back."

He stared at her, keeping a death grip on her balled-up shirt, his retreat halted by bumping into the desk. Persephone. Not Persephone. But who else had the balls to confront the Lord of Hell in his own lair?

He tried not to laugh. It was pretty damn clear this girl didn't have any balls to speak of – but she couldn't have walked through all of Hell naked like this. She'd have to be crazy.

"I've said it before and I'll say it one last time. Get out or I'll summon every demon in Hell to help me evict you. And they'll enjoy making the process as long and drawn-out as possible." He tried to make his voice vicious, but he could feel it shaking a little. He hoped she didn't notice his weakness.

She stood close enough for him to see that her eyes were the same grey he knew and loved – even if the rest of her glowed gold. There was no sign of the red that flashed in Persephone's eyes when she got angry. These eyes looked like clouds threatening rain. "Luce, they're demons. Lazy as all Hell. They'll probably bring popcorn to watch the show and back the winner. Don't get me started on the gambling in this place. Do you really want an audience? I'd prefer not to hurt you or any of the demons at your disposal. Please, just give me back my clothes and I'll leave, if that's what you really want." Her voice had returned to normal and the soft tones were nothing like those of his tattooed former PA.

Luce knew she wasn't Persephone. The nephilim didn't have sufficient self-control for this.

He wasn't sure what he'd just witnessed. The blinding light that had lit up the whole cavern as it burned the dark spirits that had plagued him since the day he'd arrived...it must've come from her. No demon could've done it. That meant she had to be some sort of angel – but angels couldn't lie. And this one had just said she'd walked naked through Hell.

She couldn't be. But if she was, she'd be furious at him even if he wasn't withholding her underwear.

One more step and her radiance would start burning him, just as it had those incorporeal dark souls. He'd had enough pain for several lifetimes and he couldn't take any more now. The sadness in her eyes hurt like Hell already.

He swallowed. "The lace on the bra is ripped," he admitted.

"It doesn't surprise me. Your fork's sharp," Mel said, her eyes straying to the bident in the umbrella stand. "Doesn't matter. It's the principle. You don't want me, you don't get to keep my underwear, Luce." She smiled sorrowfully at him.

Oh Hell – Mel had walked through Hell naked, from the front gate to his lair. For him. And then he'd made a right mess of things. Again.

A tear escaped his control, tracking down his cheek. He swiped a hand across his face, wishing he could hide it. "Mel?" he whispered.

# Forty-Five

"That's me. Now, are you going to give me my clothes back or not?" Mel's smile was pure summer sunshine as it spread across her face: fierce, but still warm. Yet her light seemed to fade and she wrapped her arms across her chest as if she was cold.

Luce shrugged out of his suit jacket, ripping off his tie, before he started unbuttoning his shirt. He paused to grab the air conditioning remote to turn the fan down. "You must be freezing," he said. "Your shirt's torn. I'm sorry.

Take mine." One of his cufflinks tinkled to the floor. He bent to pick it up as Mel moved forward.

He could feel how close she was – her foot landed beside his fingers as he scrabbled at the stone for the cufflink. He wasn't looking at the metal any more. His mind was full of perfect skin, curved over a beautiful body. The smudges of dirt and splashes of mud made no difference – if anything, they only made her more real. This was Mel, the angel he'd loved and thought he'd lost. His own body ached for hers. He dragged his eyes unwillingly to her face, letting her see his damned soul. "What if I do want you?" Luce murmured, leaving her in no doubt that he was telling the truth. He couldn't lie to her if he tried. "I know I've damned myself for eternity by killing you, but I still love you. If I could go back and change what I did, I would."

Mel smiled. "You only damaged the body I'd built. As you said, it had scars, imperfections. It took time to build a replacement. When I returned, you'd left without me. With my clothes. You should have waited – I wanted to show you Heaven." The wicked look in her eyes was far from angelic...and yet, it was.

Luce shook his head. "I'm damned for what I did. I can never leave here."

"You can and you will – I'll escort your soul through the gates myself, without wasting any time. I won't stay here, Luce. Too dark and depressing for me," Mel replied.

He wanted to believe her. Angels didn't lie. But she didn't know what he'd done while she was gone. And he wasn't willing to tell her. Right now, he just wanted to make the most of the little time he had with her, for once she found out...she'd leave without him.

"Right away? I'd have to make some arrangements here before I could just up and leave. I'm still responsible for this place, Mel – I've signed everything I could over to Persephone, but Hell is still my charge..." Luce stared at her longingly, wanting nothing more than to grab her and leave. To Hell with his responsibilities for this damned place. The demons knew what they were doing – they didn't need him to oversee them all the time.

Mel seemed to understand his longing. "It's all right, Luce. You deal with what you have to. I could probably do with a rest. I'd love a shower, but that'll have to wait 'til I get home, I guess." She looked around the bare cave, searching for something she evidently couldn't see.

Luce smiled. Here was one surprise he could offer her. "Have you never heard of Hell's bathroom?"

Mel started to laugh. "No, Luce. Hell's kitchen, yes, but your realm isn't known for its plumbing – or any water supply at all. None of the rivers here looked particularly clean. Even the air conditioning took me by surprise. What's Hell's bathroom? Some sort of sulphurous spring, a shared latrine for all the demons in the many levels of Hell? I'm sure the description will be enough for me – I don't need to smell it. I smell bad enough as it is."

"Let me show you. I swear you'll have it all to yourself. I don't share my personal apartment with just anyone," Luce said, leading the way to the wall. He rounded a corner and opened a door, set snugly into the stone. Mel laughed as she followed him through.

"I'll never get used to some of the modern things you have here. Doors in a cave?"

He shrugged. "I didn't want the air conditioning in the office to mess with the humidity in here."

Luce stood aside to see Mel's reaction as she entered. This cave was a smaller cousin of the curtain-and-column castle cave above in one of the upper levels, but this was his alone. He'd even arranged lighting so that it looked its best. He flicked the switch, letting the illumination glow into life.

Mel gasped. With her mouth still open, she turned her eyes on him. "How can you keep something this beautiful hidden in the depths of Hell?"

He stared at her, almost hurt by her shock. "What? Just because I've spent millennia running the darkest pit of punishment for the damned, with armies of demons and devils at my command, doesn't mean I don't like beautiful things. You saw the view from my penthouse. I wanted to preserve it, just for me. Not everything in my life has to be all darkness and despair."

She looked uncomfortable. "I'm sorry, Luce. I know you're more than the man in charge of Hell. I just never thought to find such beauty deep beneath so much...horrible..." She shuddered.

Luce tried to smile. "What better place to hide something beautiful? It's yours for as long as you need it. I'll be in the office, trying to get everything sorted so we can leave as soon as possible." He waved his hand and let a pile of towels appear. "Sorry, the colour scheme is a bit limited here." He concentrated hard on the stack and managed to lighten it from black to burgundy. "Will that be okay? Let me know if you need anything else."

"I'll be fine. Thank you, Luce," Mel murmured. She stepped forward to trail her toes through the water. "It's warm!"

"Geothermal," Luce replied. He looked longingly at her as she submerged into the pool, wading toward the trickling cascade. "I wish I could join you."

"I'll wait for you," she promised, closing her eyes as the water streamed over her head. A streak of gold showed through the dusty grey smothering her hair.

He hurried back to the office. He wanted to get the Hell out of here as quickly as possible – but not before he'd enjoyed a long, hot bath with Mel.

# Forty-Six

Luce buttoned and tucked his shirt in, knotting his tie as quickly as he could. He shrugged back into his jacket and picked up the air conditioning remote. He'd used the air conditioner for so long to remind him to keep his cool, but today he didn't need it. He felt like nothing could break his good mood. Mel was alive and in the next room; and when she left, she wanted to take him with her.

He dropped the remote on the desk just as Asmodeus and Merihim appeared before him.

Actually, he'd summoned three demons, not two...where was Kasyade?

He concentrated and Kasyade appeared behind the other two. He immediately tried to put as much distance between him and the two of them as he could.

"What happened to you?" Luce asked Kasyade. He'd rarely seen such injuries on a man who wasn't a professional fighter.

Kasyade tenderly patted both his black eyes and grimaced, revealing the gaps where he'd had teeth the last time Luce looked. "I met with an accident. There was an angel, you see, and..."

"Mel didn't do it!" Merihim burst out. "I blacked his eyes. Mo here broke a couple of his ribs. Should've ripped his arms off again, like he did yesterday, so he couldn't try to cheat us at poker any more. We were trying to help her. We offered her a drink, a rest, a game...tried to get her to turn around and leave. She wouldn't do it – insisted that she had to see you. So she showed us how Kas was cheating and headed through the gates of Dis into the lower levels. We told her how to open the gate. Did she make it through safely?" He looked genuinely concerned.

Luce nodded once. "She did."

"Don't hurt her!" Asmodeus said, sounding as worried as Merihim. "She...she saved me from that harpy in HR. Mel's not like other angels. We don't want her to fall like we did. She's too nice. She should stay the way she is."

"You're both attempting to tell the Lord of Hell what he should do with an angel who managed to penetrate the lowest circle of Hell, wreaking havoc on every level on her way in?" Luce kept his voice very quiet as he looked from Asmodeus to Merihim, before glancing at Kasyade. "What about you? Do you presume to give me orders, too?"

The other two glared as Kasyade and he seemed to visibly shrink, to Luce's amusement. How had he lived without Mel making everything different, by her sheer presence? She could even make a simple disciplinary meeting hilarious – not that he could let on. He was the stern Lord of Hell, after all.

"She gave me a chance to pay for cheating, without telling anyone what I'd done. I didn't listen. I didn't believe she could beat me at poker – she barely knew the rules!"

Luce thought of Mel's angelic smile, which hid more secrets than the whole of Hell. "I think Mel might be the best natural poker player this world has ever seen. I wouldn't play her unless I wanted to lose."

Kasyade grunted. "You got that right. I turned her down, she won the game, and those two beat the shit out of me and took all their money back. It was like she knew...but she wanted to save me. She acted as if I was an angel, like her. I've never met an angel like her before. It'd be sad to lose her." He shuffled his feet on the limestone, looking anywhere but at Luce.

Luce found it even harder not to laugh. How had Mel managed to charm these three demons? She'd bewitched them to the point where they'd neglected to tell him there was an angel loose in Hell – an angel who'd gotten past the gate all three of them were guarding.

He had to somehow discipline these three to maintain his authority, but for the first time, he was lost. Mel would know what to do, but he'd promised not to disturb her until he was ready to join her. Besides, what would she think of him if it looked like he couldn't control his own realm?

"I'm sending you back up to Persephone. You can be part of the new Children and Family Protection unit Lili's putting together for the latest contract." Luce glared at the three of them. "A month up there should do it."

He dismissed them.

Had he been too lenient? Luce wondered. He could have given them sword practice on Level Eight, but they were used to that. Office work and taking care of feral children would do instead.

"Next!" he called.

# Forty-Seven

Luce dismissed the last of them, wondering just how many demons Mel had met on her journey through Hell...or did she know all of them from the office? There sure seemed to be a Hell of a lot of them – and they all liked her, or owed her a favour, or both. Every senior demon knew her and had something to say.

"Don't turn her..."

"Don't press her too hard..."

"Don't hurt her..."

"Please don't change her in any way..."

"Don't be too hard on her..."

Luce's personal favourite was Ploutos' poignant plea:

"But I NEED her to make more viral cat videos! Cats from Hell wouldn't be an internet sensation if it weren't for Mel and her ping pong balls...it was like *Priscilla: Queen of the Desert* but with cats!"

Some of them even looked like they harboured romantic hopes for her, though they knew an angel would never consider pairing up with a demon.

Well, until Mel had chosen him, but Luce wasn't sure what he was anymore. A demon, an angel, some fallen hybrid between the two... If she'd have him, he didn't particularly care what he was, as long as it was good enough for Mel.

He hung his jacket over his chair, then loosened his tie and took it off. The shirt was next – he shrugged out of it and left it on the desk. She'd liked his wings before and he wanted them out for her. He looked at his pants. On or off? Would he look too eager if he walked in there buck naked, or would she think he wasn't interested if he still wore his pants?

He slowly unbuckled his belt and left it on the desk. He decided to keep the pants on – at least until he got into the bathroom. Then he'd leave all decisions up to Mel. She definitely deserved to call the shots.

He paused at the closed door, knocking lightly. "Mel?" he called. "I've finished with the last meeting for the moment. If you still want me to join you, I can come in now." He waited, but heard no reply. Perhaps she was deep in the pool, or under the waterfall. He opened the door and stepped cautiously inside.

The pool was still, marked only by the slight ripples as the cascade in the corner added to the water. Mel wasn't in the water at all – he could see to the bottom of the clear, deep pool. He scanned the room for her, his heart tightening in his chest. He couldn't lose her again.

The sound of something soft moving across stone caught his attention and it took him a moment to work out what the unusual rock formation was. Mel had wrapped herself in a towel, pillowing her head and body on a few more, and fallen asleep on the floor. The formerly red flannel was now the colour of butter, blending in with the limestone floor, so that he'd barely seen her until she moved in her sleep. She'd been bleaching his towels with her radiance, just like she'd done with his precious red handkerchief.

He'd lost track of time. So many meetings, so many demons...he'd missed out on precious time with Mel. Melody Angel. The amazing angel who'd walked naked through Hell for him, when no one else had ever willingly lifted a finger to help him. He couldn't stop thinking about it. About her.

"Melody. Sweet, sweet Melody." He wanted to take her in his arms and do every pleasurable thing he could think of to do to a woman – Hell, he'd invent a few, just for her. Luce was on his knees, reaching for her, before he realised he should probably wake her first. Not to mention ask what she wanted. The last time he'd touched her was when she'd died in his arms.

"I'm sorry I took so long," he said. "You shouldn't be lying here on the cold stone. I have a bed, you know."

"Mmm," Mel said, sighing. He wasn't sure if she was responding to him or not.

"Did you want me to take you to bed? To rest, of course. You need it."

He waited for some sort of acknowledgement, but he got none. After a few seconds, he decided to do it anyway. He'd prefer her to be angry at him for making her comfortable than to leave her on the floor. Plus, he got to carry her in his arms and lay her on his bed. Plenty of material to fantasise about later...

He lifted her body, letting the covering towel slide off to reveal her flawless skin. No, not flawless, he realised – she had a nasty wound on her shoulder, as if someone had clawed at her recently and it hadn't yet healed. When he found out who'd hurt her, he'd make sure they had time to regret their actions. A bloody long time.

Avoiding the wound, he rose and carried her carefully back to the office. The illusionary wall that hid his bedchamber – and it was a chamber, a cavern within the greater cave –

vanished to reveal the bed he rarely slept in. Black silk sheets didn't seem right for Mel, so he tried to focus on lightening the colour as much as he could before she touched them. He managed a brighter red than he had for the towels – more the colour of an open wound than a glass of rich, red wine – but there was no way he could make them as white as hers were at home.

The red seemed to suit her, Luce decided, as he laid her on silk. He stroked her hair, accidentally brushing against her hurt shoulder. She screwed her face up and grumbled under her breath.

"Who hurt you, Mel? Why didn't you just heal it?" he asked, not expecting a reply.

She mumbled something he couldn't understand, so he asked her to repeat it.

"Some harpy," she murmured. "A mistake. Won't do it again."

"Why haven't you healed it?" he asked urgently. He couldn't stand to see her hurting like this.

"Can't. Angels can't heal themselves. Healing is an act of love," she said, still not opening her eyes.

"Mel, the claws went deep. I can see where it tore muscle and..." Luce didn't want to say much more. It'd only sound gruesome. His hand hovered over the wound – he wanted to touch it but didn't dare. "We need to get you to another angel who can heal you."

"You do it," Mel mumbled.

"Mel, I can't heal. I haven't been able to heal since I fell. Only angels can..."

Mel's fingers were warm as her hand covered his to move his palm over her shredded shoulder. "You're an angel, my love. I can't think of anyone else's hands I'd like to heal me more than yours." He found he was staring into her wide open eyes. He couldn't look away. She smiled. "I'll tell you what. I'll even let you keep my underwear, if you like."

Luce laughed. "What if it doesn't work?"

She touched her lips to his fingers. "I believe you can heal me. I'll sleep better without the pain. Hell, I'll give you my underwear simply for trying. Just do it, Luce."

# Forty-Eight

He closed his eyes, summoning a power he'd been without for so long that he'd almost forgotten what it felt like. It flowed like warm water from his fingertips to his palm, heating as it concentrated. He could see the glow through his eyelids, but he kept his eyes firmly shut, concentrating on muscle and tendon, bone and blood vessel. Pain burned in his shoulder – Hell, he'd forgotten about the part where you felt the pain you took away, but for the first time in his life, he welcomed the sensation. Mel's body had to knit perfectly — she'd been damaged while trying to help him.

"You're hurting, my love. Let me take the pain away," Mel murmured. "The least I can do."

Luce felt the healing pain start to fade as her delicate touch caressed his very soul, but he resisted it. "No. You've taken enough pain for me. I deserve this." If she probed any deeper, she'd know what he'd done in his despair...and leave him. Pain was a small price to pay — and perhaps part of his penance, too.

"You don't deserve more pain, but if you wish, so be it."

Luce felt her draw back from him a little and he fought the sensation of loss that followed. She was here and he was healing her, or at least trying to...despite his best efforts, the healing warmth in his hands faded. "Mel, I'm sorry. I can't," he said bitterly, not wanting to see the disappointment in her eyes.

Her hand pushed his down, against her shoulder. The gaping hole was whole now — as if the wound had never been. Smooth and soft, an angel's skin, begging to be kissed, caressed...

Luce opened his eyes to Mel's smile. "I told you," she said. "Thank you." She leaned forward to kiss him. Long and luscious – to Luce, this kiss was as near to Heaven as he'd been in centuries. Standing at the gate didn't come close. But this was the closest he was ever going to get.

Reluctantly, he broke it. "You need to rest. I can wait – we have eternity together, or at least until this world ends." He waited for her to rest her head on the pillow again before he pulled the sheets up to cover her. He stared at the gold silk in his hands. "I'm sure this was..."

Mel laughed softly. "A joint effort, I think. Do you still think you're a demon, Luce?"

"I'm not sure what I am any more," he admitted. "Angel, demon or a bit of both."

"What makes you think there's still a little demon inside you?" she asked.

A little demon. Oh Hell. It was Luce's turn to laugh. "No, Mel. Not a little demon at all. The biggest, scariest, darkest demon you can imagine. I've heard men on Earth described as being beset by demons, but they have nothing on me, for I've been beset by, surrounded by and possessed by demons since the day I arrived here. And nothing will banish the worst one of all – because the big boss demon, the one in charge, is me. I'll always have a demon inside and that demon is me."

"Show me," Mel commanded, her voice deceptively soft.

"I don't want you to see it. It's the very worst of me – the horns, the hooves...all the darkness and horror of Hell that helps me keep order here. What an angel like you hates."

"An angel doesn't hate." Mel's eyes seemed to burn into his. "Whatever body you wear, I still see the soul inside. Show me."

Perhaps if he managed to distract her with his demonic body, she'd neglect to look too deeply into his soul. Reluctantly, Luce unzipped his fly and started pulling his pants down.

"You keep your demon in your pants?" Mel laughed.

Luce felt his cheeks redden. "No," he mumbled. "Just that this form isn't so good for clothes. You know how I said I walk around Hell naked to remind the other demons who's in charge?"

"Well, it's a relief to know I'm not the only one to walk through this place without my clothes," Mel replied. She crossed her arms over the gold sheet that hid her breasts, as if reminding him what lay beneath. "Please, continue." Her avid eyes watched him finish stripping.

"You asked for it," he said, grinning as he closed his eyes to keep that image of her face in mind. He didn't want to see her expression change to horror as his body showed her the monster that lived inside the man.

Muscles bloated and bulged as his skin hardened. The weight of his wings settled into place – leather was lighter than feathers, though most wouldn't think it. A slight air current chilled his bare head as his horns pushed their way through the stretching skin. His feet tightened, forming hard hooves. He flexed his fingers, feeling the claws extend as his teeth did the same. His mouth felt full of rocks, as it always did when he shifted to this form. He hoped he wouldn't bite his tongue in front of Mel. The skin of his back stung as his tail poked its way through, point first. He drew a breath into his expanded lungs, feeling the power in this body. He was the Lord of Hell – and he was afraid to open his eyes to see what Mel thought of him.

He heard the light slap of her feet on stone as she approached. Would she keep going, running past him and all the way back up to the surface, to Heaven where she belonged? Or would she have the courtesy to say farewell first? Luce clenched his fists, squeezing his eyes shut tighter still.

# Forty-Nine

Gentle fingers trailed up his spine, stroking the soft membrane between his wing digits as she somehow soothed away his fears. "This body has harder skin than the form you usually wear. I miss the plumage, but your wings feel so delicate when they're bare like this. It's hard to believe something so fragile can carry your weight, let alone anything else." Her lips touched his back, between his shoulder blades. "You're so much hotter in this form, too." She sounded amused.

Impulse drove him to whirl around and whisk her into the air, wings beating as he shot upwards with her. He'd never thought of his demon body as big before, but she seemed so small in his arms as they soared high above the Styx and the walls of Dis.

Mel placed her hand over his heart and the beat quickened for her.

"So much suffering in one place," she murmured sadly, surveying the scene spread below her. Her hair felt tantalisingly soft against his skin as she laid her head on his chest. Luce breathed deeply, savouring her scent. "I don't know how you can stand it."

"I belong here. This is Hell and I am the lord of this place. Torture, torment and all the despair I can't stomach. I can never be an angel again for you, Mel. Behold, the demon!" He threw his arms wide, releasing her.

He expected her to cling to him in fear, or fall into the Styx below, so he'd have to catch her. How many times had he underestimated Mel?

"Not all angels fall, Luce." Her wings shone far too bright for this dark space, seeming to give off their own light as they fluttered gently to buoy her. Her hand remained on his chest. Her touch was so light it might have been the feathers in her wings instead of her fingers. Mel lifted her head to look into his eyes. "You're not a demon and you belong with me," she said, smiling.

Luce wanted to believe her, but the evidence wasn't looking good. "Angels don't have horns or tails or wings without feathers...and they don't have claws, either."

Mel's white wings lifted her higher than Luce. Her lips touched the top of his head, right between his horns, as she treated him to a lovely, close-up view of her breasts. Angels probably don't get this horny, either, Luce thought, enjoying what was offered so freely.

Her eyes met his again as she sank a little lower. Luce froze as he felt her reach around behind him, her fingers drifting down his lower back, one vertebra at a time, until they closed around him completely. He stared at her as her hand slowly stroked the length of his tail, stopping only at the tip, which she brought to her lips.

If there was someone he could have sold his soul to so that she'd continue, he'd have done it on the spot.

"The Lord of Hell does, for he has a reputation to maintain with the demons he rules. The body you wear is not a representation of the soul inside – merely what is appropriate for the time and the circumstance. I know you, Luce." Her words echoed in his head as she took his tail-tip in her mouth, sucking it like a spoon of that chocolate raspberry mousse she'd loved.

Oh God. Did she know how many nerve endings she'd just electrified with one stroke of her tongue, arcing up his spine to his euphoric brain?

Luce felt like he was going to burst out of his pants. If he'd been wearing pants...well, she'd be under no illusions that his body enjoyed the attention. He clenched his eyes shut so she wouldn't read the desire consuming his soul. She'd already read deeper than anyone else. "How can you possibly think you know my soul? I killed you once. The darkness you didn't see could rise and do it again." Sweet torment as her tongue tantalised his tail. She would have made as good a demon as she did an angel. With an effort, he wrenched his tail from her grasp, trailing the damp tip down her cheek, her throat, caressing her skin as he moved the point slowly down.

"Because my soul is bonded with yours," she whispered.

Horrified, he jerked away from her. "No, Mel. I never asked for your soul. Never wanted to damn you with me to this place..."

She sniffled and smiled as she lifted her head, wiping her tears away with careless fingers. "Of course you didn't. You came to me and asked for my help. I shared it with you freely. I breathed my spirit into you, expecting your demon spirit to fight me and carry you home to Hell to escape from being burned by the brightness of mine. But there was no darkness shielding you from me – instead, your soul welcomed me in with...with love." She swallowed as an untended tear trickled down her cheek. "How could I respond with anything else? I felt the bond form – surely you did, too! – and when we parted, the connection between us remained. It helped me find you, but it doesn't hold me here. My soul is still my own – just linked with yours."

Luce swallowed painfully. "If...if that's true, I didn't know about any bond. If I'd known you were in Hell, searching for me, instead of dead or in Heaven...I wouldn't have...I wouldn't have..." He'd thought he'd heard her voice, encouraging him to hold on when he'd wanted to die, but that was easily dismissed as wishful thinking.

"Show me," she said softly.

Fateful words.

"You don't want to see," he whispered, as the horrors came unbidden. The despair that drove him to his own weapon, ripping flesh, bleeding on the floor...and waking to Persephone, as he lay puddled in his own blood. Saying Mel couldn't...didn't...would never love him.

Falling. He plummeted into darkness again. This time, strong hands caught him. No one had ever...no one...yet he was rising. Mel. How could she bear his weight as well as her own? Her fragile wings were smaller than his, but together they ascended.

"Hold on, Luce. I'm so sorry. I should've come sooner. Left clearer signs. Like the one at the entrance. Didn't you see?" she entreated through her tears.

Red glitter. Not Michael. Mel. He closed his eyes. "I thought it was someone else, trying to torment me by reminding me of you. I never thought you'd come here for me. That you'd want to..." He stared at her, not even sure how to finish his sentence.

"I've never...I never wanted to bond with anyone before. You...I've read so many souls, but I've never tried to share what lies in mine. Please...tell me if this reaches you." Mel closed her eyes tightly and frowned as she attempted whatever it was she meant to do.

He watched her but felt nothing. "It's all right. I'm probably not perceptive enough to pick up on..."

"Oh, to Hell with it," she exclaimed and kissed him. Leathery lips, mouth full of fangs, forked tongue and all.

Her love burst upon him like a depth charge, leaving him breathless. How could her body hold all that feeling in? All for him. "Mel," he choked out, desperate not to hurt her even as her tongue caressed his. His mouth was a bloody booby-trap for him – he was terrified he'd bite her. God knew he'd bitten his own tongue often enough.

"A demon would feel unbearable pain from my first touch and I didn't hurt you," Mel said, licking her lips. Her tongue looked miraculously unhurt, too. "You're no demon, my love."

"No," he agreed. He became uncomfortably aware of where they were. "How about we take this back to my office, instead of in front of an audience that includes half of Hell?"

Mel surveyed the hundreds – perhaps thousands – of demons and damned souls who were looking up in what might have been the first time in millennia. Self-consciously, she folded her wings. "Yes. Please, take me down, Luce."

Holding as tight to her as he had during their ascent, he mirrored her smile. He had her all to himself, now without an audience, and she loved him. His hooves had barely touched the stone floor of the cavern before he kissed her deeply.

"I don't deserve you," he said.

"You didn't deserve centuries in Hell. I hope you might consider what I have to offer some small consolation for what you've suffered."

"Hardly small, Mel," he murmured.

"There's something else that isn't small..." She glanced down, blushing. "I can certainly see why you intimidate the demons so much in this form."

He'd never been glad of his red skin before, but he was now. She didn't see how his blush burned darker than hers. "I'm not normally this big," he insisted. "It must be because I'm so close to you. You could help me relieve the pressure a bit..." He pressed hopefully against her.

"Luce, you're huge," she protested before he cut her off with another kiss.

He concentrated on bringing his body back to be the man she'd known on Earth. Perhaps he had overdone the size of his demon body a bit...but it had all been proportionate. When his claws retracted, Mel didn't seem so small any more. Secure in his arms, she felt...perfect.

"When I leave here, I want you to come with me," Mel said, bringing him back.

He found himself, lost in her eyes. "That sounds wonderful." It took him a few moments before he added, "Hop on and I'll take you anywhere you want to go." He sat on the bed and patted his lap.

Mel laughed, shook her head, and sat beside him instead. "Heaven. I want to take you home to Heaven with me, Luce."

Luce wanted to drop everything on the spot and go with her. Even to Heaven, if that's what she wanted. He opened his mouth to offer.

Someone started beating down his door. "Lord Lucifer! I need to speak with you!"

Mel shrugged. "You're still the Lord of Hell. I bet you have a fair few demons who are wondering what exactly you were doing with the strange angel."

He pulled on his pants and stood up. "I'll let you rest. If you need anything, I'll be in the office next door, working as hard as I can to get the Hell out of here as soon as possible. With you."

She smiled, nodded, then sighed and settled deeper into the pillows. A thin silk sheet covered all he wanted in this world and he hoped he'd never have to give her up again.

# Fifty

Luce concentrated on concealing the chamber where she rested with an illusory concrete wall once more. She didn't deserve to have demons staring at her as she slept.

When she was hidden from sight, he waved the office door open to allow the knocking nuisance entrance.

He leaned on the desk, doing his best to sound stern even as his thoughts were still flying with Mel. The doorway stood empty. "Well? What's so urgent? Have you decided you don't need to speak to me after all?"

The old ferryman, Charon, stepped hesitantly inside. His approach was painstakingly slow and he seemed to consider each step before he took it. Almost halfway to the desk, he stopped, lowered his hood and said, "Lord Lucifer, I came to ask about...the lady."

The lady. Mel was all that and more. "What about the lady?"

Charon twisted a fold of his robes in his hands. "The lady...I wanted to ask if she was safe and well."

Luce stared at the man. "I don't see what it has to do with you. My business with the lady is hers and mine alone. Now, did you have something to tell me or not?"

"Lord Lucifer, I do need to tell you something," Charon admitted. "You can't keep Lady Muriel here. She belongs on Earth, not in Hell."

So the old ferryman knew her, though he'd never met her in the office. Had Mel managed to charm him here? Luce tried not to laugh. "Aren't you going to tell me not to try to turn her? That's the first thing everyone else said."

Charon choked out a laugh. "You've got to be arrogant or stupid to think you can best her – and your arrogance always was legendary. Lord Lucifer, not even you can turn Lady Muriel. She's one who'll never fall. She's too sure of her path. And you'll have every angel in Heaven and on Earth come looking for her if you keep her here much longer. You can't hold the Domination of Heaven and Earth and Hell."

For a moment, Luce was reminded of Michael. "What does my fall have to do with Mel? Michael said that, too – but he wasn't talking about Mel. He was talking about..."

Charon howled with laughter, almost doubling over in mirth. "You're a fool, Lord Lucifer. You mean you didn't know..."

"Well met, ferryman," Mel said softly. She stood before the illusion of a wall, draped only in a gold sheet. Luce's fingers itched to tear the sheet away from her body so he could see her in all her glory. "You never gave Luce my message that I was looking for him. You could have saved me a lot of time and a fair bit of trouble if you had."

Charon's chin jutted out, showing his Adam's apple as he swallowed nervously. "I still hoped you'd turn back, Lady Muriel. This is no place for you, and I worried that he'd keep you as he tried to turn you. The world needs you above, not hidden away here, until he gave up."

Mel strode to Luce's side. "Luce knows he can't keep me here and I won't stay long. He will come with me."

Luce stared into Mel's eyes. She was right. Of course he would. How could he not?

Charon started to laugh. "I didn't think it was possible for an angel to fall twice. Michael will have a fit when he finds out."

"He already did," Mel admitted. "But he knows he's powerless to do anything about it."

"You two are talking in riddles," Luce grumbled. "This is my office and I'm supposed to be in charge of this place."

"Is he?" Charon asked Mel. She smiled and nodded. He turned to Luce. "Do you know who leads the choir of Hashmallim?"

"Sure," Luce responded. "That's...Raphael,

the archangel who's Mel's boss at the agency. He led them into battle against me when..."

"No," Mel interrupted. "It's me, Luce. Raphael acts as my second in charge. He insisted that we needed to be present at the battle and he begged to be the one to lead them. Boys and their battles – I wouldn't stand and watch that idiocy. He took those who agreed with him. He left me a lot of work to do and no angels to do it. No wonder I summoned both you and Michael to Earth to speak to me when I found I couldn't leave." She looked almost angry. "If you'd bothered to accept my invitation, I could have saved you a lot of pain."

Luce shook his head. "I didn't get any message from you, Mel. Never. I swear..." His memory gave him a kick. "Wait. One of the Grigori brought me a crazy message he said was from Michael. It made me laugh. Something about how I should go down to Earth before offering battle and beg some girl to help me..." He stared at her in horror. "Mel, I'm sorry. If I'd known..."

"You've paid your penance, Luce. How

many centuries have you served here? All you had to do was ask for my help and you finally did, on the floor of my little house. And Michael said you'd never find me, the Domination of Heaven and Earth, in such plain surroundings."

Charon coughed. "I'll be going. Don't linger too long, Lady Muriel. The world needs you above, and soon."

Mel smiled. "Oh, I know."

# Fifty–One

Luce repeated the old ferryman's words and saw in Mel's expression that she knew his thoughts, too. Hell, she knew his soul. How could she not know what he was thinking?

"I was sent here so that I'd never have the Domination of Heaven and Earth. Set upon by that bloody sword, forced to fall against my will to land, shattered, HERE. I wanted to prove that arrogant angel wrong. I could have control of Earth in legal contracts, because humans are stupid and they'd do anything for money. All along...the Domination of Earth wasn't a vague concept. It was YOU?" Luce kept his voice level for most of it, but the line of reasoning seemed too preposterous to be true.

"Yes. The Domination of Earth is me and...Michael believed he was protecting me. If you sought my help...he foresaw that I would enter Hell." Mel's words were quiet and careful.

"So he hid you. For centuries, he's hidden you. How could you go along with it? He sent me here – forced me to fall. Every other angel had a choice, yet I had none. And what was my crime? That he feared I'd take you from him?"

Mel bowed her head. "They told me that you wanted me to guide you, and you alone. That you were evil and would use me for your own ends, which would not match mine. Michael, Raphael – those who witnessed your fall – they said you would confine me in Hell; that Michael had seen that in my future. If you found me, asked for my help...I would come here and you would never let me go. So I did what I had to – and hid from you. I can see the currents of future events – all bar those that involve me. I could only trust the foresight of others. I'm sorry."

Luce's voice died and what came out was a hoarse whisper. "I didn't know you. I didn't know who you were or how important you could be. I never hunted for you, never wanted to hold you against your will. I never knew your name until you told me, Mel. I swear I never would have wanted you to share my fate – confined to a Hell you didn't deserve." He stared into her eyes, willing her to read his soul, if she hadn't already. "Please, believe me. I had no idea of any of what Michael accused me of wanting."

"I didn't understand what he'd done until outside the gates of Heaven, Luce. They wouldn't even use my true name. Lying in your arms, I saw it all...but the only place I could make amends was in Heaven. I let my damaged body disintegrate and headed home to straighten out the tangled mess Michael had made. And when I returned to tell you...you'd gone. How could I not follow you into Hell? An innocent man has no place here." Mel looked determined. "I want you to come with me, to walk triumphantly into Heaven. To show them they were wrong. About you. About me. But only if you're willing."

Luce snorted. "Mel, I've committed most of the sins the damned are in here for. Suicide. Murder. Betrayal. Lust. Bad counsel...and that's just this week. No one in their right mind will let me into Heaven. I should apply to Minos for my level assignment here..."

"Angels aren't perfect, Luce," Mel began.

"DON'T!" he snapped, breathing hard. "She...she said that. Angels aren't perfect, they're just better than everyone else..."

Mel's eyes turned hard. "Persi. I'm going to have some serious words with that girl when I see her next. She should never have come here..." Her gaze softened. "She was misquoting me, Luce. I told someone once that angels aren't perfect, but we try to be. That's what sets us apart. The soul I see inside you belongs in Heaven. Perhaps not in the highest ranks of angels yet, but we all have to aspire to something. They won't keep you out with me at your side."

Luce managed a grin. "And you'd stay at my side this time? What if we run into more crazy, weapon-wielding mothers?"

Mel's smile spoke of untold power. "Ah, but I have nothing and no one to hide from any more. They'll face Lady Muriel of the Hashmallim and not just Melody Angel. What I did to those dark souls here is nothing compared to what I can do."

"And the gatekeepers – Michael with that damn sword and the dude in the dress?" Luce persisted.

"They wouldn't dare challenge me if they have to acknowledge my rank, and they will." Mel held out her hands to him. "Come to Heaven with me, Luce. You offered to show me Heaven once, on Earth. While that was wonderful, I can show you a time far more sublime in Heaven." Her wicked grin returned.

"How can any man refuse an offer like that?" Luce replied. "When do we leave?"

Mel looked down. "After I've had another bath. It looks like I missed a bit of mud before...and I'm not taking any part of Hell home with me."

# Fifty-Two

Before he left, Luce had one final matter to attend to: finding the harpy who'd attacked Mel so he could make the bitch pay.

Lili gave him a searching look as she led two other harpies into his office. "I take it you're feeling better?" she asked, glancing around.

"I have no idea what you're talking about," Luce replied.

She smiled. "So you've broken the new toy I sent you already? Impressive."

Mel. She thought he'd harmed Mel and she

seemed happy about it. Was Lili the one who'd attacked his angel? Surely not. Lili wouldn't have sent the girl to him if she'd already damaged the goods. But she'd seen Mel, so she must know something.

"Time for an update on Level Seven. Do you have any issues to report?"

Lilith, Jezebeth and Ananiel exchanged glances but didn't seem to want to respond.

"I heard Level Eight's looking for more personnel again. I'll volunteer all three of you until someone else more appropriate chooses to take your place," Luce offered lazily, watching all three and wondering which of them would break first. One of them had to know who'd hurt Mel.

"The heating system's not operating as well," Jezebeth volunteered. "Meg on Six must've turned one of the graves into a hot tub again. I wouldn't mind if she invited us, but she only invites men, and when she's done with them, she boils them alive. I don't see why she has a hot tub and we don't."

Luce nodded, scribbling down notes. "I'll send one of the engineering demons to take a look. The pipes might just need replacing again. Anything else?"

Lilith cleared her throat. "We need replacements for some of the barbed whips. They seem to wear out far faster than the smaller floggers. I'm not sure if it's overuse or poor workmanship."

"More whips, too." Luce scrawled another line. "Anything unusual?"

"There are rumours that the illusions on Level Two have failed and the place has turned into a mass orgy," Jezebeth said, glancing at Ananiel. "Right, Ana?"

Ananiel glared at her. "I wouldn't know anything about orgies or Level Two. I've been working hard in Level Seven the whole time."

Jezebeth burst out laughing. "The Hell you have! For the last two days, you've been practising double stuffing on Two with any men that'd have you. I heard you even had the new fallen angel twins – at the same time! I'm surprised you can walk after all that sex, let alone work. No wonder you just mess with the women on Seven, and the little ones, at that, like the one you carved up today – you're too spineless to dominate a man."

It was Ananiel, Luce realised. She'd attacked Mel.

"I do my fair share of torturing damned souls!" Ananiel shrieked. "You take the floggers home to use on your horse of a husband. I've seen you! Just because I don't have a permanent partner, you're making me look like some sort of slut!"

Lilith sighed. "Ana, I counted twenty-five men yesterday and thirty the day before that. You don't need any help from the rest of us to make you look promiscuous. All you have to do is open your skinny legs. Lord Lucifer doesn't need to know about your insecurities. I'm sure I can reassign you to work in the office on the surface if you wish. You can go back to running your little illegal brothel in the disabled toilets at the food court, in between hiring more office whores for the CEO to bend over his desk."

Luce wondered when they'd be finished with their silly spat. Hell, he could hardly believe he'd accepted Ananiel's services or that of any of her stable of office girls. After Mel, he couldn't contemplate even touching one of them again, least of all the crazy Ananiel. His thoughts strayed to Mel, behind that door, who'd be lovingly soaping that sweet skin of hers, like a perfect, living statue in his private pool. And she was waiting for him to finish so he could join her. He couldn't wait.

Silence fell and Luce dragged his eyes back to the bitching harpies. "I'll be shifting the suicides to Level Eight for clean-up duty. They're not much use to you on Seven, are they? That'll give you more space for usurers – we seem to be getting a Hell of a lot of them the last few centuries. Does that work for you, Lili?" He stared at the harpies – now reduced from three to two. "Where's Lili?"

"She left," Jezebeth replied. "Can we go, too? I have another six souls to torture today and Ana's behind again."

Luce considered this before saying, "I'll speak to the imps about the issues on Two. Ana, you're confined to Seven and if I hear a single tale about you turning the tables on the damned souls so that you're the one being tortured, I'll send you down to Eight permanently. This is Hell. Damned souls aren't supposed to enjoy themselves. Now get back to work." He waved them away and both harpies hurried out.

Alone, Luce had an important decision to make: to join Mel now or be responsible and sort out Level Two and the imps first? Luce knew what he wanted, and it most definitely involved Mel. Duty or one Hell of a lot of pleasure? Such a tough choice.

# Fifty-Three

Mel lingered to enjoy the cool cascade over her shoulders for just a little longer. She would simply have to find similar bathing places on Earth, if she could. Small streams created such cascades the world over, surely – she'd never paid them much attention before. She thought about seeking some out in Korea – though she'd settle for hot springs in their cold climate – and wondered if she should take Luce with her. Perhaps it was too soon for such things.

She thought she saw movement out of the

corner of her eye and called out, "Show yourself. If you were after a glimpse of my body, you've had time to grab an eyeful as I travelled through Hell. I have nothing to hide."

A shadow stepped from behind a column. "You've certainly been showing off, angel. You have the male half of Hell talking about you, and a fair few of the women, too. No one can believe an angel would cross Hell just to see its lord."

Mel strained her eyes to recognise the face that matched the familiar voice. "Lili?"

The red-skinned female demon who stepped into the light resembled Lilith, though any sign of humanity was gone, as was evident in her clearly visible horns. "Did you think you were the only woman he's had here? There's something about him in the water that's made so many female angels fall that I lost count a long time ago."

"I don't need to count," Mel replied with a smile. "It's all in the Book of Judgement, outside Heaven's gates. Over a hundred and fifty thousand, I believe, though perhaps he didn't bring all of them here." She shrugged.

"As long as I don't have to bathe with them all, I don't mind."

"He's not yours. He'll never be yours, because he's always loved me," Lilith snarled.

"Who?" Mel asked, confused.

"Lord Lucifer. He's mine – has been for millennia. I've stood by his side through the centuries, his right hand and his partner in all his grand plans. He'll discard you when he's done using you, yet another fallen angel...just like all the others. So fresh-faced they hardly recognise who he is before he's turned them into his personal playthings. That's when he throws them away – to be harpies in Hell, or errand girls in his office." Lilith stepped to the edge of the pool, dipping her hoof into the water. "He's mine," she repeated.

"No," Mel said softly. "He's...his. Luce is his own man, neither yours nor mine. Demons can't love, Lili. He can't have loved you. I'm sure he's grateful for all your help and your companionship through so many dark years, but he couldn't love you. And you can't love him."

"You know nothing, you little angel bitch!"

Lilith screeched, launching herself at Mel. The demon was so fast, she blurred as she hurtled through the air.

# Fifty-Four

Sighing, Luce decided to deal with work before he joined Mel. Hopefully, he'd have longer to spend with her, without interruptions. What demon would dare invade his personal bathroom?

He summoned the imps' leader, then sat back to wait. Despite their appearance, he never mistook them for demons – they were his allies. How in Hell was he going to keep them amused now that he only wanted Mel? Even the thought of those voyeurs watching him with the woman he loved put him off. Especially as they communicated in a form of soul-to-soul telepathy. The thought of them in his head was worse than them watching him and Mel.

"Greetings, Lord. Where sexy Lady?" Sptlk's amusement coloured his soul-voice.

Luce's mind immediately brought up the delightful picture of Mel's naked body submerging in the pool. He quickly shut it down, not wanting Sptlk to see her naked or to know his weakness for the angel.

"Lady safe. Wish to offer respect. Will wait."

The imps had never offered him respect, Luce reflected, but quelled that thought quickly, hoping Sptlk wouldn't catch it. "I don't want to discuss Mel. I want to ask about the illusions on Level Two. There are reports that the damned souls are without illusion on that level. Can you confirm?"

Sptlk's amusement increased. "Illusions gone. Orgy entertaining. Many hours, many souls. Many demons, too. Many thanks to Lady for spectacle. Debt now owed."

Luce tried to wrap his head around this.

"Are you saying Mel dispelled your illusions? Before Mel instigated an orgy?"

"Lady order. We obey. Much amusement. Lord learn from Lady for eternal loyalty."

The graphic pictures Sptlk conveyed showed an intimate knowledge of Mel's body as well as some of his own fantasies, Luce realised with horror. The imps had watched him and Mel when they'd...oh, she'd kill him if she knew. Gaining the imps' eternal loyalty wasn't worth losing Mel if she found out he'd let them watch the couple make love.

"Lady already knows. Imps cannot hide from Lady. Lady sees through all illusion. Gracious permission from sexy, seductive Lady. Honour for us. Great honour for you. Redemption, too."

They knew. The imps had helped him disguise his soul for centuries – hiding it behind an illusive shroud so thick that none could penetrate it – so that no one else could know that his was the only soul in Hell that wasn't completely tainted by malicious shadows.

"I need the illusions restored on Level Two

and the shroud around my soul must remain, for no demon can know I'm not one of them. Can you do it?" Luce crossed his fingers. He knew he didn't need to ask for their price – Sptlk would show him.

The imp flashed his pointed teeth in a wicked grin. "Can, yes. Will, if Lady does not order otherwise. Lord must pay reparation to Lady for disrespect." Pictures flowed through the Sptlk's mind, each more detailed than the last, showing Mel's impassioned face as Luce pleasured her body in every way he knew how.

"She won't let me do that," Luce said hoarsely, unable to get the erotic images out of his head. If Mel let him do any of those things, he'd be in Heaven.

"Kneel and beg." Sptlk laughed and disappeared.

Aching for the angel, Luce strode across the office toward the private pool where Mel and Heaven awaited.

# Fifty-Five

Mel languidly lifted a dripping hand and Lilith splashed into the pool. Mel sighed and waded through the water to the edge, stepping onto the limestone beside her bath. The demon charged through the water at the angel's unprotected back, her claws out and ready to rake.

"No," Mel murmured, turning and holding up her hand again.

Lilith stopped in her tracks, one hoof raised to take a step that she couldn't complete.

"What have you done to me, bitch? This is some trick. A new angel like you doesn't have the power to stop me like this. Even if he'd turned you, you couldn't!"

Mel shook her shoulders, the rippling movement flowing into her wings as they faded into sight.

"What in Hell? Those aren't real!" Lilith hissed.

Mel turned sad eyes on the angry, immobilised demon. "Lili, I did everything you ever asked of me in the office. You, of all people, can hardly doubt my angelic patience. Even an archangel would have snapped at least once. But I never did. You owe me more favours than the rest of your corporation combined – and, one day, I will collect. I always do. As for the power to stop you...I can, and I will. Even here, I hold greater power than your lord. I am Muriel, leader of the Hashmallim, and I have come for him."

"Bullshit," Lilith spat. "The leader of the Dominations is Raphael. Everyone knows that. I've never heard of a female Domination."

"Do you remember Luce as an angel, Lili?

When his wings were white?" Mel asked gently.

"His wings were never white. They were blacker than the night sky when he came to me. He sought solace in my body and I gave him everything. My life and my heart. He loves me, angel. You lie."

"You were human," Mel breathed. A tear slipped down her cheek. "Then you can never understand. Angels don't lie. And demons don't love. If he met you after he fell, he was no longer capable of love, Lili. He's deceived you for centuries, if he told you he did." She sniffled and struggled to smile. "He had the biggest, whitest wings of any angel I'd ever seen. I only saw him once, when I was in Heaven on business. He breezed past me, deep in conversation with two other Seraphim. I don't think he even saw me. I thought he was an arrogant prick then, too."

Lilith struggled, but after a few seconds, she burst out laughing. "Yeah, he's an arrogant prick, all right." She seemed to calm a little as realisation crossed her face. "If he can't love me, you know he can't love you, either."

Mel smiled sadly. "But he does, Lili. It

almost destroyed him as half his soul fought the other part of itself. I had no idea. He gave up everything to find me, because he thought I could help." She hesitated. "I did what I could. I had to help. Angels always do." She bowed her head. "I'm sorry."

Lilith's expression hardened again. "Not as sorry as that bastard will be."

The door swung open and Luce stood in the doorway, beaming. "Mel, my love, I'm finished. May I join you?"

Lilith let out a scream of rage and Mel released her in shock. The enraged demon launched herself at Luce.

# Fifty-Six

Mel looked miserable, Luce thought. Were those tears on her cheeks, or just water from the pool?

Weight and pain hit him all at once. Something sharp seared his shoulders as he fell back against the floor, cracking his head on the stone. The blow blinded him, so he couldn't even see his assailant.

"Mel?" he gasped out. He tried to fight off the crazy, clawed beast, but its frenzy lent it more strength than he felt he had.

He got his hands around the creature's neck and squeezed, trying to crush the air out of it so it would stop.

"NO!" Mel shouted.

Luce felt the weight lift off him. Blinking through his pain, he saw the red, clawed creature suspended above him. He stared at it and it stared back.

"Lili?" he asked, mystified. Why would his most loyal lieutenant attack him?

"You're a fucking lying bastard, Luce, and I should never have trusted you. I'd give anything, never to have met you!" she screeched.

"Lili, I..." Luce struggled to sit up, but the pain in his head made him wince. What he saw of his chest was a mess of blood and ripped flesh. Lilith's claws had dug so deep she'd shredded skin and muscle. It made Mel's shoulder wound look like a slight scratch. He could see his own ribs and some of the organs beneath. Wait, was that his...

Mel's feet made no sound on the stone. She was simply there, kneeling beside him. "Shh, let me." She laid her hands on his chest, stroking the stinging wounds, and the burning started to subside. Mel lifted her fingertips to his temples, and his blurred vision cleared. "You have blood everywhere, Luce. I need to get you to the pool to wash it off." Luce felt his body leave the ground, floating on nothing.

"What the Hell?" He started to struggle, trying to find what, if anything, was supporting him.

"Luce. Just hold still," Mel murmured. He felt air on his skin as his clothes vanished, before it was replaced by cool water. Wavelets lapped the pool as Mel's gentle hands sluiced water over his chest. "It's in your hair, too. Immerse yourself completely – duck your head under for just a moment."

"What did you do to him? Why is his blood red? Did you turn him human, angel?" Lilith demanded, her voice shaking. Her red face had paled to pink in what Luce thought might be fear.

"He's taken his true form – that of an angel, as he originally was. Not as powerful as he was, or I am, but an angel, like me. One who is capable of love," Mel said. "It was his choice."

"And what about me, Lord Lucifer? Do all these years of service mean nothing?" Lilith spat at Luce.

Love and Lilith – now there were two concepts that didn't go together. He'd repaid all her services with his trust, as he let a former human rise in the ranks so that she was on the same footing as the senior fallen angels. What more could she possibly want from him than the power she so ardently craved? He didn't know how to answer her, so he continued to stare.

"I'm done, Luce. You should probably get dressed," Mel said.

He dragged himself out of the pool and began to put on the clothes that Mel had left on the floor. He gave the shirt up as a loss, but his pants were intact. "What about you, Lili? You just tried to claw my heart out of my chest." He coughed and it bloody hurt. Perhaps she'd punctured a lung before Mel had patched him up. "I'm sure we have a circle in Hell reserved for souls who betray their sworn liege lord. I think it's a particularly nasty one, too."

"So demons can't love and angels can't lie? What can you do now?" Lilith asked bitterly.

"Demons don't love. They fuck and form alliances – that's all. You chose to become one. I never forced you." Luce shrugged.

Lilith flexed her claws and reached for Luce. "Are you just going to leave me hanging here, angel?" she demanded. "Let me down!"

"Are you going to try to hurt him again?" Mel asked.

"He seduced me with promises he couldn't keep, lied to me for centuries! I deserve retribution!"

"I understand your anger, but you deserve no such thing. You chose your fate and he's served his penance. Heaven accepts his contrition, Lili – you should, too."

"Go to Hell, angel. I don't want your pity or preaching. You've turned the Lord of Hell into a lapdog. Take him to Heaven and castrate him – see how long you can keep him then! Leave and let me down."

Mel nodded. "You've made your point clear, Lili. If I ever see you again, it will be to collect what I am owed. Nothing else." She turned a smile on Luce, who finished buttoning his pants. "Let's go, Luce." She held out her hand and he took it.

# Fifty-Seven

Soft cloud formed beneath his feet as a gentle breeze caressed his freshly healed skin. He should be wearing a shirt, he decided, concentrating. No, a whole suit. This was definitely a formal occasion. Maybe even a tie...no. A shirt unbuttoned at the throat looked far sexier. Such a pity all he could manage was black.

"What do you think?" he asked Mel.

She smiled as her eyes wandered across his body. How did she do that? The longer she looked, the more turned on he became. Oh God, he was going to walk into Heaven with a hard-on. Hell was one thing, but here...

"You need your wings, Luce. This is one of those times when appearances count. You're making an entrance that no one dreamed was possible. Make them remember who you are – the angel Lucifer, Lord of Hell." Mel's voice was mellifluous, her warmth melting the icy fingers that clutched at his heart.

He hesitated. "Wings and shirts don't go so well together. I always end up ripping things. Ripped clothes won't work if I'm trying to look impressive."

"Like everything in this place – your body, your clothes, all of it – your wings and your clothes are simply an illusion. It's all about appearances." She reached for his chest and tapped a shirt button, which glowed gold. Mel smiled. "Even the blood my body shed the last time we were here was an illusion."

It had seemed so real – Hell, her blood had even tasted real. He couldn't lose her again. He wouldn't lose her again. He seized her hand and spread his wings. He breathed deeply and prayed that this time, for the first time ever, he'd be allowed happiness.

The breeze ruffled his feathers as Mel's musical laughter rang out. "As if I needed more feathers," she said, so quietly it was barely audible. "I'd forgotten how heavy they are."

Luce looked and looked again, just in case he'd been mistaken. He didn't remember her wings being quite so wide – surely they were bigger than his! She flapped them twice, her feet leaving the cloud beneath them as the powerful lift carried her body with it. She was still laughing as she drifted down, folding her wings neatly behind her. Her pearlescent skin glowed from within as Mel turned her dazzling smile on Luce.

"If it's all right with you, I'd prefer not to give fuel to the rumours that I walked naked through Hell for you," Mel said.

Luce's heart dropped faster than she had done, just moments before. "You're ashamed of what you did for me? Even I can't believe you did it. I want to see the faces of some of those righteous angels when they realise what you've done..."

Now Mel's smile was serene. "I don't regret my actions for a moment, but it might be easier for the angels and souls waiting for judgement if I have some clothes on, is all. I'm sure they'll all hear the truth and it will only add colour to the legend. Most of them won't notice the angel beside you, but if they do, it might be best if my arse is covered. Like this, we look like something off the cover of one of Lili's dark erotica books — the CEO in a suit, with a scantily clad young woman at his side."

Luce grinned back. "Well, if you put it like that...if you're going to wear sexy lingerie, I think I'll be walking behind you to take in the view, instead of beside you."

"Then I'd best be a little more modest," Mel said softly, closing her eyes. A shimmer began over her breasts, cascading over curves to dim her steady glow, so that her skin was merely glittering instead.

Luce blinked and managed to miss the final step that set her transparent dress opaque, but it was the colour that arrested his attention. She wore the gold silk dress he'd seen in her wardrobe, clinging to every curve as if it loved her as much as he did. His knees went weak. He was going to kneel and beg, the moment he got her all to himself in Heaven. "I thought you wore white," he said.

"I did, and sometimes I still will," Mel responded, glancing down. "I like the simplicity of being Melody Angel, but your escort must be Lady Muriel. My time for hiding is done. Today it's time for a show of power, and an angel of my rank must be clothed in gold." She lifted impish eyes to his face. "I need to look good enough to be seen with you, Luce. I believe the human term is arm candy."

Luce leaned in close so that his lips brushed her ear. "You know that'll make me think of how sweet you taste, every step of the way."

"As long as you look impressive, your thoughts can wander wherever you like," Mel replied, turning her head to claim a kiss. "Are you ready, Luce?"

He released her reluctantly, so that their only contact was their joined hands. "As I'll ever be."

Together, they strode forward.

# Fifty-Eight

A billow of cloud blew aside with a flutter of Mel's wings. Now he could see the crowd that awaited them – the benches bridging the gap between them and the Book of Judgement were full of angels and some saintly souls, too. Far more than on the day they let Mel die.

Mel wouldn't die today, Luce swore. At the slightest hint of trouble, they'd both fly and to Hell with the consequences.

His eyes kept straying to their audience. There were very few wings in sight, and none as magnificent as Mel's. Even his stood out, both for their colour and size. Perhaps he should have thought to wear something lighter – a grey shirt and suit, instead of his customary black. He wasn't sure he could do anything about the colour of his wings.

Luce glanced at his sleeve, which looked a little lighter. He focussed harder on the fabric, willing it to change.

"Relax, Luce," Mel murmured. "I won't let anyone hurt you."

He laughed. "I was thinking that I should've worn a lighter shirt."

"Let me help you with that." Her voice was barely a whisper, but he heard it clearly. Her hand landed on his thigh and stroked up his side to his shoulder before caressing his arm.

Under her lingering fingers, his sleeve shifted a few shades lighter still. He glanced at the seated souls and their escorts to see if they had noticed the change. He couldn't catch anyone's eye, he realised, watching each of them look down as he passed, as if they were afraid to lock gazes with him. Just like that innocent little escort last time – the one who'd been terrified of him. Now Luce dropped his own gaze to his feet. His pants were dark grey, he noticed, but the lightening colour wasn't enough to lighten his heart. He didn't belong here.

Mel stopped, and, touching his cheek, she looked into his eyes so that he could see the love that filled her soul. "Don't forget that you're the angel I love, claiming your rightful place at my side in Heaven. Every angel here aspires to what you have. Do you want them to remember you as the arrogant angel who strode into Heaven, the miracle of redemption no one believed possible, or the broken demon who was beaten by a girl and dragged back here?"

Luce couldn't help it — he burst out laughing. "Which would you prefer me to be?"

"If I wanted to drag in a broken demon, would I have given you a choice?" Mel whispered. "Though I think we could make quite an impression if you go for the red, bulging muscles and I fly in, with you hanging from my hand by one huge leg..." She glanced down, smiling wickedly. "I think you might intimidate angels as much as demons that way – but it's not particularly dignified. Best if you keep your pants on, I think."

"I love you, Mel. Lucifer the arrogant angel, at your service." He straightened his shoulders and lifted his chin, sensing her merriment but not daring to catch her eye or they'd both laugh. She knew him better than he knew himself. He'd had centuries of practice being an arrogant demon – an arrogant angel couldn't be much harder, surely.

They continued past the line of benches and he tried not to look at the watchers any more. All that mattered was Mel and their destination.

Luce fixed his eyes firmly on the gates as they grew larger with every step he took. Glowing pearl and not steel; the base of the bars shrouded in misty cloud. Today his misgivings were gone – today they would swing open more smoothly than the stone gates of Dis. Somehow, Mel had infused him with her certainty. He prayed for her to be right.

Mel drew him to a halt beside the gate

guard, who still wore a white dress. The angel bowed deeply. "Welcome home, Lady Muriel. I think I speak for every angel in Heaven and Earth when I say we're relieved to see you return, safe and sound."

"Did you really think I wouldn't, Peter?" Mel asked gently.

He straightened so he could face her. "Many of us were worried for you. When you ventured where no angel has returned from...and you, an angel we could scarce do without...we feared the worst. To see you return, with the one you said you'd save...I am in awe, Lady Muriel." He bowed again, this time from the waist. "May I be the first to congratulate you on your conquest of Hell?"

Luce laughed so hard he almost choked. Mel and whose army? She'd have had to bring all the forces of Heaven to Hell and she couldn't conquer the whole place without defeating every single senior demon in addition to himself. Lilith would never give up without a fight – nor would any of the others, if only out of pride.

"You make it sound like some sort of

violent battle. I merely travelled through Hell to help Luce and bring him here," Mel said softly, her now-watery smile melting Luce's heart. Mel wasn't the conquering type.

Movement caught Luce's eye on the edges of his vision. Those on the benches were standing and bowing, too – all in Mel's direction. Even he felt compelled to pay her the same homage. They hadn't been avoiding his eyes at all, he realised – they'd all been showing their respect to Mel.

Mel's fingers tightened around his and Luce lifted his head to look at her. She'd turned pale and the smile that lifted her lips was nervous and uncertain. She'd stayed on Earth, avoiding this kind of attention for centuries. Yet when she'd had a message to convey in front of a pack of human reporters in the office, she'd frozen and fallen to her knees in tears. The indestructible angel who'd fearlessly taken on all the forces of Hell and won...suffered from stage fright.

Luce slipped an arm around her waist and pulled her close. His now-white sleeve disturbed her feathers, marring their perfection, but she didn't make a sound of protest. "You don't know how happy I am that you did. How about we get the gate, Mel, and leave this bloke to deal with the backlog of work he has queuing up?"

Mel nodded jerkily and allowed him to lead her to the shimmering portal to Heaven.

"So, how do we do this?" Luce asked, looking at the bars preventing his passage.

Mel smiled wanly. "At least we don't have to play a game of poker to find out. The same as your gates to Dis – the touch of an angel."

"Well, do the honours then, Melody Angel," he replied with a flourish of his hands.

"No, together. We do this together," she insisted, her voice still small but gaining a little volume as it stopped shaking. She held tight to his hand, stretching her left hand toward one gate as he extended his right toward the other. "Now."

Her delicate hand and his larger one touched the bars at the same instant, sending the gates swinging wide open to permit them both passage into Heaven. With their hands still joined, they stepped forward together.

He could feel her shaking, but she continued to take one step after another and he kept pace with her until she stopped. Mist swirled around her bare feet, making his light grey trousers look even lighter beside her creamy legs. "If I asked you to turn my wings white as well as my clothes, would you do it?"

"No," Mel replied. "Only you can change those and the colour is a part of who you are. You're still the Lord of Hell, as well as an angel, Luce. That makes your wings...quite striking, as well as unique." Her smile seemed genuine again. "Besides, you know how I feel about dark wings. Think of the swans." She stretched out her fingers, caressing his feathers. He didn't want her to stop, but he didn't want to embarrass her in front of the audience.

Luce glanced back to see if the crowd at the gates were still watching them, but they, the gates and everything outside of Heaven were no longer visible. He sighed his relief, understanding why Mel had relaxed.

"Congratulations, Luce. You're the first fallen angel and the first redeemed demon ever to enter Heaven. I'm honoured that you let me be the one to escort you this far." Mel's expression glowed with joy.

Centuries...millennia...they'd kept him out. No more – all thanks to Mel. "Thank you," he managed to say before he grabbed her, crushing her wings in his fierce hug. He kissed her next, repeating his thanks when she broke for air.

He could have gone on kissing her forever, but she disengaged from him gently. As if to offer some compensation for the end of kisses, she clasped his hand between hers.

"So, what do you have in mind for your return to Heaven, Luce? What would you like to do first?" Mel asked with a smile.

Luce eyed her hungrily. "I want to do you first. All this about how it'll be better in Heaven...I want to see for myself. And I really, really want to use these." He produced the handcuffs from his pocket. The very special new ones that featured in his favourite fantasy about Mel.

Mel cleared her throat, her eyebrows lifting almost to her hairline. "You're finally redeemed, allowed to enter Heaven for the first time in centuries, and the first thing you want to do is handcuff me to a bed and..." Her hands seemed to convey quite eloquently what she failed to find the words to express.

Luce chuckled. "No. These are for me. Lady Muriel, illustrious leader of the Dominations, I was hoping you might..."

"I hardly need handcuffs to hold you anywhere I want you, my love." Mel's smile turned decidedly wicked. "Maybe later, if you like. First, I think I should show you how angels do it in Heaven."

# Fifty-Nine

Luce woke from his blissful slumber and untwined himself from Mel. She may not have conquered Hell, but she'd conquered him so completely he never wanted to be apart from her again.

Something kept nagging at his mind. The old ferryman, asking if he was still the Lord of Hell, but he'd been looking at Mel.

And she'd nodded...

She'd have had to defeat all the senior demons in Hell in order to conquer the place.

But Mel didn't work that way. Her style was more subtle – persuading them all to mutiny in her favour, perhaps.

By all that was holy...she had. Geryon, Merihim, Kasyade, Ploutos...even Lilith.

He cuddled up to Lady Muriel, conqueror of Hell. It's not like she'd needed to go to so much effort, he mused. He'd give her anything and he'd go to Hell and back to get it for her. All she had to do was ask.

"Lady Muriel. Lady Muriel. Please forgive the intrusion, but Michael sent me. Raphael said it was urgent..."

Surely she'd earned a longer rest than this. Evidently not. Reluctantly, Mel unwound herself from Luce's embrace. "What is it, Jehannette?"

"It's Persephone. She's disappeared."

Mel felt Luce's interest arouse. "She has? That's wonderful news!"

"No, it isn't," Mel said gently. "I know you

don't like her, but I need to see her. Raphael was supposed to bring her to me for a meeting regarding her recent conduct in Hell. If she's disappeared, then who's running the HELL Corporation?"

"That's her problem, not mine any more. I gave all that up, remember?" Luce cuddled closer to Mel.

"You signed it over to the agency, not her personally. If she's not taking care of the company, it falls to Raphael," Mel replied. She turned to Jehannette. "How long has she been gone? Does he have a suitable caretaker?"

"I don't know, Lady Muriel. Both archangels told me I needed to find you, tell you the news and beg for your help." Jehannette's barely-contained panic said more than her words.

Mel relaxed as she said, "Go tell them that I'll return to my little house on Earth as soon as I can. I'll find her and make sure the corporation is well cared for."

Jehannette hurried off, her relief as visible as the cloud beneath her.

"I still don't see how it's your problem," Luce grumbled. "Don't go. Think of all the trouble I'll cause, up here alone without you."

Mel drew away from him completely, feeling bereft already at the slight parting. "That's why you're coming with me, Luce. We'll return to HELL together. Just think – you'll get to wear pants again."

# ABOUT THE AUTHOR

Demelza Carlton has always loved the ocean, but on her first snorkelling trip she found she was afraid of fish.

She has since swum with sea lions, sharks and sea cucumbers and stood on spray drenched cliffs over a seething sea as a seven-metre cyclonic swell surged in, shattering a shipwreck below.

Demelza now lives in Perth, Western Australia, the shark attack capital of the world.

The *Ocean's Gift* series was her first foray into fiction, followed by her suspense thriller *Nightmares* trilogy. She swears the *Mel Goes to Hell* series ambushed her on a crowded train and wouldn't leave her alone.

Want to know more? You can follow Demelza on Facebook, Twitter, YouTube or her website, Demelza Carlton's Place at:

www.demelzacarlton.com

# Books by Demelza Carlton

## Siren of Secrets series

Ocean's Secret (#1)
Ocean's Gift (#2)
Ocean's Infiltrator (#3)

## Siren of War series

Ocean's Justice (#1)
Ocean's Widow (#2)
Ocean's Bride (#3)
Ocean's Rise (#4)
Ocean's War (#5)
How To Catch Crabs

## Nightmares Trilogy

Nightmares of Caitlin Lockyer (#1)
Necessary Evil of Nathan Miller (#2)
Afterlife of Alana Miller (#3)

## Mel Goes to Hell series

The Devil's Work (#1)
See You in Hell (#2)
Mel Goes to Hell (#3)
To Hell and Back (#4)
The Holiday From Hell (#5)
All Hell Breaks Loose (#6)
The Devil Goes to Heaven (#7)

## Romance Island Resort series

Maid for the Rock Star (#1)

The Rock Star's Email Order Bride (#2)

The Rock Star's Virginity (#3)

The Rock Star and the Billionaire (#4)

The Rock Star Wants A Wife (#5)

The Rock Star's Wedding (#6)

Maid for the South Pole (#7)

Jailbird Bride (#8)


## Romance a Medieval Fairytale series

Enchant: Beauty and the Beast Retold

Dance: Cinderella Retold

Fly: Goose Girl Retold

Revel: Twelve Dancing Princesses Retold

Silence: Little Mermaid Retold

Awaken: Sleeping Beauty Retold

Embellish: Brave Little Tailor Retold

Appease: Princess and the Pea Retold

Blow: Three Little Pigs Retold

Return: Hansel and Gretel Retold

Wish: Aladdin Retold

Melt: Snow Queen Retold

Spin: Rumpelstiltskin Retold

Kiss: Frog Prince Retold

Reflect: Snow White Retold

Roar: Goldilocks Retold

Cobble: Elves and the Shoemaker Retold

9 781925 799019